SNOWFLAKE'S GIFT

BY LINDSAY MCKENNA

Blue Turtle Publishing

Praise for Lindsay McKenna

"A treasure of a book... highly recommended reading that everyone will enjoy and learn from."

—Chief Michael Jaco, US Navy SEAL, retired, on Breaking Point

"Readers will root for this complex heroine, scarred both inside and out, and hope she finds peace with her steadfast and loving hero. Rife with realistic conflict and spiced with danger, this is a worthy page-turner."

—BookPage.com on Taking Fire
March 2015 Top Pick in Romance

"... is fast-paced romantic suspense that renders a beautiful love story, start to finish. McKenna's writing is flawless, and her story line fully absorbing. More, please."

—Annalisa Pesek, Library Journal on Taking Fire

"Ms. McKenna masterfully blends the two different paces to convey a beautiful saga about love, trust, patience and having faith in each other."

—Fresh Fiction on Never Surrender

"Genuine and moving, this romantic story set in the complex world of military ops grabs at the heart."

—RT Book Reviews on Risk Taker

"McKenna does a beautiful job of illustrating difficult topics through the development of well-formed, sympathetic characters."

—Publisher's Weekly (starred review) on Wolf Haven
One of the Best Books of 2014, Publisher's Weekly

"McKenna delivers a story that is raw and heartfelt. The relationship between Kell and Leah is both passionate and tender. Kell is the hero every woman wants, and McKenna employs skill and empathy to craft a physically and emotionally abused character in Leah. Using tension and steady pacing, McKenna is adept at expressing growing, tender love in the midst of high stakes danger."

—RT Book Reviews on Taking Fire

Also available from
Lindsay McKenna

Blue Turtle Publishing

DELOS

Last Chance, prologue novella to Nowhere to Hide
Nowhere to Hide, Book 1
Tangled Pursuit, Book 2
Forged in Fire, Book 3

2016
Broken Dreams, Book 4
Cowboy Justice Bundle/Blind Sided, Bundle 2, novella
Blind Sided, BN2
Secret Dream, B1B novella, epilogue to Nowhere to Hide
Hold On, Book 5
Hold Me, 5B1, sequel to Hold On
Unbound Pursuit, 2B1 novella, epilogue to Tangled Pursuit
Dog Tags for Christmas Bundle/Snowflake's Gift, Bundle 3,
novella
Secrets, 2B2 novella, sequel to Unbound Pursuit, 2B1

2017
Snowflake's Gift, Book 6
Never Enough, 3B, novella, epilogue to Forged in Fire
Dream of Me novella, epilogue to Broken Dreams
Trapped, Book 7
Taking a Chance, Book 8, sequel to Trapped

Harlequin/HQN/Harlequin Romantic Suspense

SHADOW WARRIORS

Danger Close
Down Range
Risk Taker
Degree of Risk
Breaking Point
Never Surrender
Zone of Fire
Taking Fire
On Fire
Running Fire

THE WYOMING SERIES

Shadows From The Past
Deadly Identity
Deadly Silence
The Last Cowboy
The Wrangler
The Defender
The Loner
High Country Rebel
Wolf Haven
Night Hawk
Out Rider

WIND RIVER VALLEY SERIES, Kensington

2016
Wind River Wrangler

2017
Wind River Rancher
Wind River Cowboy
Wind River Wrangler's Challenge

Dear Reader,

Welcome to the Delos Series! *Snowflake's Gift* is a stand-alone novella, because sometimes, a character just comes to me and says, "Hey! Tell my story!"

And I love all animals, but horses, dogs and cats are my pet favorites (sorry for the pun!). But this story is about military vets coming home from war, too. I am a Navy veteran myself, active during the Vietnam War (I stayed in the USA, providing rear support as a meteorologist).

I also love Christmas stories about love and happily ever after. These are the reasons I wrote this heartwarming novella. We can all use a lift during the holidays.

Nick Conway, US Army WMD dog handler, has spent years in Afghanistan saving the lives of troops. First with Dude, his yellow Labrador and then with Snowflake, an Australian shepherd. He's released by the Army due to PTSD. Coming home is a relief and yet, he feels guilty about it. He has only been home for a few weeks, helping his mother out at her diner in Hamilton, Montana, when his life changes for the better.

Holly McGuire is a Delos Charity owner in Hamilton. She takes care of many of the town's elderly shut-ins who can no longer feed themselves and need other types of services and help. At twenty-five, she has seen a lot of tragedy, so her work to make those less fortunate a little happier, feeds her soul.

When Holly meets Nick in the dishwashing area of the diner on that fateful September day, it is Snowflake who brings them together. Broken and depressed, Nick discovers hope in Holly's sunshine smile and dancing blue eyes. Santa Claus has a surprising gift in store for both of them, thanks to Snowflake's gift!

I'd love to hear what you think about my Christmas novella, the Culver family, and the Delos Series! Don't be shy about contacting me via my website at www.lindsaymckenna.com. And Happy Holidays!

Dedication

To Tricia Speed, who does it all. I couldn't do it without her!

CHAPTER 1

September

NICK CONWAY GAVE his Australian shepherd, Snowflake, a fond look as he deposited the dirty plates, flatware, glasses, and cups in the industrial-size dishwasher. Snowflake was lying on his favorite red-cotton blanket in the corner of the Yellow Rose Diner's back room. The dog tilted his head, intuitively aware of his master's gaze, and adoringly rested his blue eyes on Nick.

"It would sure be nice if you could come up here and help me with these dishes, partner," Nick suggested with a grin. In response, his ex-Army WMD dog panted in the September heat. To give them some relief, Nick had opened the back door to let some fresh air in. Damn, this washing-up room got hot, despite the air conditioning. It had snowed three days ago, but the white stuff had melted quickly, and now the Indian summer temperatures raced to eighty degrees during midday and then dropped below freezing at night. Fall in Montana was mercurial at best.

His mother, Sue Conway, who was now forty-six, had run their family-owned diner since she was twenty-years-old and pregnant with him. The lunch rush had just ended and Nick was still learning his duties as the new dishwasher.

Outside, he could see what was known as the Bitterroot Valley, surrounded by the Bitterroot Mountains. They already had snow on top of their craggy peaks, their blue, granite flanks covered with snow, which tended to come early to this part of western Montana. The diner sat nestled within a beautiful panorama of the valley, with the Bitterroot River winding nearby. It was a trout fisherman's paradise and Hamilton was a favorite haunt of hunters and fishermen, as well as winter sports enthusiasts.

But being back home felt like a big comedown after being in the US Army as a dog handler, saving men's and women's lives all over Afghanistan. Now, he reflected on how many pointless deaths he'd witnessed, how many close calls he'd had, and the long term effect of the loss of his first WMD dog, Dude, a male yellow Lab.

By helping in the kitchen, he could earn money to pay for an apartment of his own within a month or two. Although the military now paid for his college education, the checks would arrive after he'd completed his studies, not before. That meant he had to have a paying job to allow him to leave his parents' house and find a rental somewhere else.

Okay, so being a dishwasher wasn't what he'd dreamed of after he was released with an honorable medical discharge, thanks to a stubbornly recurring case of PTSD. But still, it would pay enough to keep him going for now. His black brows dipped as he finished off the huge plastic tubs filled with dirty dishes, feeling pride in his work. He wouldn't always be doing this, but for the next two years, he'd treasure this menial part-time job. He was grateful his mother had offered it to him after he'd told her he would like to find another place to live.

Nick tugged off his green plastic gloves, dropping them onto the nearby aluminum counter. He grabbed a fresh cloth and began wiping down the shiny, aluminum surfaces and appliances around the washing room. Everyone was glad to see the lunch crowd go as they went into dinner preparation mode. The eager diners would begin to arrive from five p.m. onward.

His mother would wait tables occasionally, taking orders when there was a surge of hungry tourists during summer vacation. But right now, the kids were back in school, and it was an older crowd of regulars who stopped in for a friendly meal.

This was his seventh day on the job and he wanted to make his mother proud. Nick was happy to have this type of low-stress job and be able to help his family in the process. His PTSD didn't allow him to work in high-pressure situations where he'd have to deal with lots of people. That kind of environment could aggravate his cortisol levels and raise his anxiety. A dishwashing job was perfect—it was just him in a back room with a door he could open for fresh air when he needed it. He also had time to attend all of his college classes and to do homework.

The ability to have an "exit point" was important ever since Dude had died while following the trail of an IED. It had led to an Afghan goat barn with a thatched roof, Nick was holding the Labrador on a sixteen-foot leash as they entered the stable area. Set up as a trap, an IED went off, killing Dude instantly and knocking Nick six-feet backwards. He had been rescued by his comrades, who found him unconscious and badly bruised, but thankfully, still alive.

That had been a black day he relived again and again. Thank God they'd given him Snowflake after his return to duty. The two had bonded immediately. Snowflake would also start when a car backfired, or when someone shot a gun. He would wince and duck his head upon hearing those very sounds. Yes, his best friend had PTSD, just like him.

Around Hamilton, everyone was a hunter and owned a gun or two. As a kid growing up here, Nick hadn't been bothered by the sound of gunfire, but now, the sound of guns made him crouch down. There had even been times when he'd dive down to the ground, convinced he was under attack. Snowflake reacted similarly, depending upon how close the shots were being fired. They were quite a pair, Nick thought wryly. He loved this dog with the same intensity as he'd loved Dude.

As Nick cleaned up the last batch of dishes that his mother had just brought in to be washed in the next load, he tried to focus on his job. His mother had earned an A rating for her diner and was very proud of it. Lately however, her chef, Tony, had shrugged off safe-food preparations. Nick knew his mother was a stickler for proper food care—and with good reason. She was actually relieved when Tony had stalked off last week in a huff. Now, she was the cook for the diner until she could hire someone else.

Nick wanted to ease his mother's stress, so he volunteered to help with washing up. It didn't take a brain surgeon to figure out how to use the industrial dishwasher after she gave him a quick run-through on how to use it. As a kid, he had cleared tables at this diner, cleaned them, and taken the dishes and cutlery back here. That was how he'd earned a weekly allowance. Being here in the washing-up room wasn't all that bad—it brought back some memories that he actually found comforting.

"Hey! Hello! Is Tony here? May I come in?"

Nick, who'd had his back to the screen door, jumped, then whirled around. Snowflake instantly barked a greeting, his short tail-stub wagging.

Surprised, Nick saw a young woman with curly red hair. She was standing on the top step, smiling up at him. His heart was hammering because she'd scared the hell out of him! Trying to appear calm, he told Snowflake to go back to his bed in the corner, which the dog did reluctantly. He too, wanted to know who this cheerful, freckled stranger was.

Pushing open the screen door, he said, "Tony quit last week. I'm Nick. Can I help you?" She had big, blue eyes that danced with such life, he realized how damn long he'd missed seeing that kind of glint in a woman's eyes. In Afghanistan, women's gazes were flat, dark, wary, and sometimes, filled with hatred toward Americans. This young woman was like a breath of fresh air rushing toward him.

"I'm Holly McGuire," she said, thrusting out her hand. "I run the Delos food charity over on Main Street. I'm here to pick up any leftovers for this week's dinners for the shut-ins I take care of." She craned her neck, looking around. "Are you their new dishwasher?"

He released her hand, feeling its amazing softness. "Yes, I am. Come in, please. I'm not sure where Mom keeps that extra food, but hold on a minute and I'll get her."

"Oh," Holly said, "no worries. I know exactly where it is. In fact, I have some large, cardboard boxes to bring in so we can put all the cans and plastic containers inside them. Would you like to help me?" She gestured out the door to her white van. "The boxes are out there. Tony used to lug them in and out."

Nick followed her outside. "Sure, I'm happy to help."

Snowflake rushed out the door, right on Nick's heels—after all, they worked together as a team. As Nick walked with Holly, he noticed how the mid-afternoon, September sunlight glinted on her burnished hair. Was she of Irish descent, he wondered? The thick strands were mussed, caught up in a large, maroon comb at the back of her head. It suited her. He liked the way the fall breeze made the curls dance around her oval face.

"Handsome dog," she said, halting at her van. "What's her name?"

"This is Snowflake—and he's an Australian shepherd," Nick pointed out.

Snowflake pushed in between them, panting,

gazing adoringly up at Holly who leaned over and gently patted his head.

"Oh, he's beautiful! I've never seen a dog like him. I love the color of his eyes. I never realized dogs could have blue eyes."

"That's standard for the breed," Nick offered. "He was Army trained to search for WMDs in Afghanistan. I was his handler."

Holly's fresh-scrubbed, freckled face became somber. "Oh wait," she said, straightening, "are you Nick Conway? Sue's son, who was in the Army? Gossip around town a few months ago said you were finished with your enlistment and you were coming home."

Nodding, but not wanting to get into the unpleasant details of his release, he simply said, "Yes, I'm Sue's son, Nick. Where are your boxes? I'll carry them in for you."

Holly had a beautiful mouth, he decided. She was maybe around his own age, slender, wearing a set of tan, corduroy jeans, and a long-sleeved pink tee, plus hiking boots. Holly looked outdoorsy, not like someone who ran a charity. Looks were deceiving, as Nick well knew.

"Oh . . . the boxes. Sure, they're in the back of the van. Just open up the doors," she said, following him.

Nick opened the van's squeaky, protesting doors. The vehicle was badly rusted, probably at least ten-years-old, the fenders eaten away by the salt used on the roads every winter. He assumed the van was well-used as a charity vehicle, and that Holly probably didn't have much spare money to put into it. He picked up two large, sturdy cardboard boxes. Holly waited patiently for him to bring them out, then picked up the other two.

"I can get them," he protested over his shoulder.

"Oh no, that's fine, Nick. I can carry them!" She flashed him a wicked grin. "I've been doing this for the past four years, since I was twenty-two."

He hesitated, waiting for her to catch up, and then opened the back door to the diner. She went to a prep table he'd just wiped clean and set the boxes down. She certainly looked twenty-two— so fresh and untouched in her tailored jeans and pink tee-shirt.

Unlike himself. He'd seen the changes to his face when he shaved—he was gaunt, his green eyes murky and dark. He was beginning to resemble those Taliban soldiers with their lifeless gazes. That realization alone scared the hell out of Nick. He didn't have the guts to tell his parents that he felt like a robot, totally numb, without feelings. He'd been that way for the last three years of his deployment.

"Did you just get home?" Holly asked, going to one of the huge refrigerators and opening it.

"Yeah, two weeks ago."

She turned, smiling at him. "Thank you for your service, Nick. And Snowflake, thank you for yours, too," she said, ruffling his fur. Then, she quickly washed her hands with soap and water and began to sort through some huge, plastic containers inside of the refrigerator.

"Thanks," he said, moved to hear her appreciation for him and his dog—who really did the life-saving over there.

"I imagine it was a shock coming back from Afghanistan," she said, taking six, half-gallon round plastic containers out of the fridge.

Frowning, he stood awkwardly, not sure what to say. "It always was," he managed.

"Your mom is an angel. I hope you know that." She tucked the containers in the first box, going back to the fridge for more. "When I got here at twenty-two, I was pretty lost. I was having a coffee here at the diner, and she came out of the kitchen to ask me why I looked so sad. I was a stranger who had stopped in after having recently lost my parents in a car accident. The driver was texting while the car was going eighty, and he ran them off the road. Their car turned over and they died. The other driver survived without a scratch."

"God, I'm sorry," he said, really meaning it. He saw her eyes cloud with grief.

"Thanks," she whispered, stopping for a

moment after shutting the second fridge. "Your mom asked me what I wanted to do with my life and I told her I felt so lost, I had no idea. She pointed out that there were a lot of elderly people, shut-ins, here in Hamilton, and she was doing her best to bring them leftovers from the day's cooking, but she couldn't do it all by herself. And the shut-ins couldn't come to the diner, although Sue does feed those who can walk over here for a decent meal. Your mom doesn't charge them a dime. You're so lucky to have her."

"I remember her telling me when I was overseas that she was trying to get the elderly to come over here. She's a strong believer that we're all family, Holly, and my mom considers all the people of Hamilton her children and her responsibility."

He watched as Holly nodded, moving quickly and confidently, filling all those boxes full of food as they chatted.

"Oh, that's so true, Nick! We sat there for hours talking, planning, and figuring out how we could feed Hamilton's elderly and the poor children who weren't getting three meals a day."

Hearing her made him yearn for his younger days, before he'd joined the Army. He'd been as idealistic, hopeful, and brimming with energy as Holly was right now. But that was then . . .

"Mom did mention in an email that there was

a Delos charity coming to town. Is that your gig?"

"Sure is! Your mom knew about Delos. They have a shut-in program here in the U.S. for the elderly who can no longer shop or cook for themselves. Shortly after speaking to your mom about Delos, I flew to their Alexandria, Virginia headquarters and talked to Dilara Culver, their CEO. She's just the best role model in the world! We spent two hours in a boardroom with her staff, who helped me organize and set up the plan so I could feed the needy here in Hamilton. I came back here with a mission." She moved to another table holding ten loaves of bread, which she placed in another box.

"Does Delos pay you to do this?" he wondered. Charities usually consisted of volunteers.

"Indeed they do. I get a monthly check based upon how many people I'm feeding on a daily basis. They give me another check for my work hours, which also helps pay other business expenses, like part-time employees and the cost of certain fresh vegetables and fruits. Your mom volunteered her diner and Delos sends her a check monthly based upon what she's giving the elderly. I think that's more than fair for everyone. I come in every five days about this time to pick up the containers of food. Your mom has me sign a paper listing all the items, their cost, and I send it back to Delos. I just love working for

Delos."

"Do you have help?"

"Well," she hedged, "yes and no. When my folks died, they left me enough money in their will for me to buy that old motel at the edge of town."

"Oh, the Kingston Motel?"

"Yes, it looks a lot different now. Dilara sent in a construction engineer and she, and her team, went through the entire two-story building, redesigning it for things that I'd need for the charity. By the end of the reconstruction, I had ten rooms left over. Dilara suggested I rent them out to people who couldn't afford the usual rent for an apartment." She smiled. "As you know, Hamilton is a tourist town. It's our only source of income. There were a lot of people who couldn't afford the usual rents, especially during the long, winter months when their money dried up after summer jobs were over." She shrugged, "What could I do? If someone can pay the low rent, I let them live there. For those who can't, I ask them to pitch in and help me, either in our kitchen, or around the charity. I always need help making a huge pot of soup every day, and cooking meat when I can get my hands on some. There are three people who do upkeep on the building, clean it, pick up trash, and one guy who's a jack of all trades. He takes care of the plumbing and electrical matters when they arise. Everyone gets paid for their contribution."

"It's very kind of you to do all this," he said, not quite believing someone as selfless as his mother could actually exist. Holly reminded him of a youthful fairy godmother, and his heart warmed to that image. She was cute, pert, and bursting with life. Nick wished he could absorb some of her idealism, but he knew it had been burned out of him forever. "Do you have any rooms to rent right now?"

"Funny you should ask," she said, picking up one of the boxes and holding it, "I do have one apartment available. Could you open the door for me? I have to get all these boxes out to the van."

Nick wondered where the hell his manners had gone. "Sure, hold on," he said, quickly moving to the screen door and pushing it open. "Tell you what," he offered, as she walked down the concrete steps, "I'll bring the rest of the boxes. They're heavy and you shouldn't be hefting them around. You're just a little thing."

Laughing gaily, she turned at the bottom of the steps, grinning up at him. "Little but mighty, Nick Conway. Don't you ever forget that! I might be small, but I'm all heart."

There were so many replies to her statement he couldn't speak, so he just shrugged and said, "You take the box with the bread in it. I'll get the rest. And I'll accept no arguments." He turned and heard her lilting laughter drift across the parking lot. For the first time in a long time, he found himself smiling, and even more amazing, he felt warmth flooding his chest. It was such a strange awareness that for a moment, Nick froze, holding the big box in his arms as he stood on the steps.

Was it possible? Could Holly's winsome smile and the deviltry dancing in her eyes make him feel something again? Stunned, Nick stood there for a moment trying to absorb what had just happened. Ever since Afghanistan, he'd been numb. Now, this red-headed, elfin sylph with her warm, down-to-earth grin seemed to hold a key to a reserve of feelings he hadn't known still existed. Could he escape the paralyzing, icy darkness of a prison that had held him captive for years?

HOLLY TRIED TO focus on making the ten plates of food for her shut-ins in her charity kitchen, but she couldn't help but wonder if Nick Conway felt that charge that had leapt between them from the moment they met. She swore she felt as if lightning had struck her dumb for a moment because he'd looked at her so intently. It felt as if he already knew all about her. That was wild! And totally unexpected!

As she scooped out big dollops of warm,

macaroni and cheese into each of the ten aluminum containers, her thoughts refused to settle down. Yes, she'd known that Sue Conway had a son in the Army. Yes, years ago she'd shown Holly his photo. At the time, Holly had thought that Nick was terribly handsome, but the man she'd met less than an hour ago was very different. He looked much older than his age, his eyes resigned. Now, he had lines at the corners of his eyes and slashes on either side of his mouth.

It wasn't surprising, of course. Not after all that time in war zones. His physique was impressive, though—he looked more like a surfer dude: lean, hard, and exquisitely honed, setting off a happy dance for her hormones.

As she finished her ten aluminum plates, she put the empty plastic food containers in the sink, turning on the water to wash them out. Normally, Myra Berringer, a woman in her fifties, did the kitchen work here, but she was out sick today, resting in her apartment. Holly had quickly organized the mac and cheese, coleslaw, a fresh, warm roll, and steamed green beans with onions and bacon in each aluminum container. Sue Conway's cooking was beloved by everyone in Hamilton and her shut-ins could hardly wait to see what surprises and goodies she'd concocted for their evening meals.

Best of all, Sue had made a special pan of pineapple upside-down cake just for them, and

Holly quickly put it in another small container, snapping down the plastic lid on each one. Luckily, before Myra went to lie down, she'd put out ten, large paper sacks, with napkins, salt, and pepper in a small zippered bag for each elder.

Holly gathered together a large, plastic urn of fresh, hot coffee and another one filled with hot tea. In ten minutes, she'd brought all of it down to her white van parked just outside the kitchen door. It was 4:45 p.m., and she'd be right on schedule for her first shut-in, Beth Bolton, at five p.m. It took her nearly two hours to give out the ten hot meals to her ten shut-ins because each stop involved more than dropping off food. She would stay at least five to ten minutes, chatting with each elder, finding out about their state of health, and any issues that might have arisen since she'd last seen them. Once that was accomplished, Holly would hug her shut-in, tell them goodbye, and to stay out of trouble, which always got them to laugh.

Holly cared deeply for her elderly clients. She'd known them ever since she'd arrived here. They were her cosmic family. Tomorrow, a registered county nurse, Hilary Carter, would be coming to town to give each of them a medical checkup. This was done every three months. Holly had all their medical information in a big file drawer in her office. She would bring them along, listen to the nurse, check all prescriptions, and miss nothing if she could help it. There were a million small details to pay attention to on a health visit, and it was times like this that she wished she still had her driver, Oscar Duarte, but he'd passed quietly in his sleep two weeks ago at the age of seventy-five.

She really needed a new driver. Nick had asked about renting out an apartment here at her charity. Maybe he could drive and help her daily with her shut-ins as trade for a room. He had looked hopeful when she'd told him she had an opening, but she hadn't really had time to give him any details.

Nick, she realized, was haunted. It was the only word that truly fit him, the look in his eyes, the energy around him. He was tense, as if waiting for a bomb to go off nearby. As she made her stops, she stole moments trying to feel her way through this enigma of a man. Holly couldn't explain why she was so drawn to him, either. She had to admit it—she was always a sucker for an underdog who was having trouble coping with life. It brought up a lot of painful memories for her.

But there was much more going on. She was no longer in a relationship. A year ago she broke up with her boyfriend because he was disgusted by the elderly people she cared so strongly about. James Westmore was an accountant in Hamilton, twenty-eight, and superficially sophisticated. He often looked down on the poor and helpless, especially older people, impatient with their physical and mental slowness. She'd often seen disgust on his face, and Holly hated his coldness toward everyone, regardless of their age. He wasn't exactly a good lover, either, and her lips turned up over that last thought. He was a taker, not a giver. He wanted to be pleased first, and she always came second. This was not what Holly wanted in a man. She wanted a full partner, not to be a slave to a man's selfish whims. She had walked out on him and never looked back.

What kind of lover might Nick be? She sensed that he would be a tender lover who would treat her as his equal. Maybe she saw it in his eyes—she wasn't sure. Maybe it was her woman's intuition, which was pretty good most of the time. The fact that his eyes turned gentle when he gazed at Snowflake, his dog, was a good sign. A man who loved his dog that much was one she'd like to know better.

There was so much unsaid and unknown about Nick, and her curiosity about him was eating her up. Holly had made her last stop and was on her way back to her base of operation, giving her time to think more about this quiet, intense man. Sue had never said much about her son, perhaps because Nick wasn't sharing much of anything with his mother. Her own background gave her more wisdom about combat,

PTSD, and what it did to a human being than she'd ever wanted to know.

Chewing on her lower lip, she placed the van in park, locked it, and climbed the stairs up to her second-floor apartment. It was dark, the stars so bright she felt like she could reach out and touch them. Unlocking the door, she saw that the lights in the kitchen on the first floor had been switched off. Myra had probably come in, despite feeling ill, cleaned up, and shut them off. Holly would check in on her before she fell into bed, exhausted.

Throwing her keys in a glass bowl sitting on the foyer desk, she hurried to her bedroom to change her clothes and get comfy. Her favorite attire after hours in the cold season was an old pair of gray gym pants and a long-sleeved gray top. Then, on went her soft, wool slippers that hugged her ankles. She walked out to the kitchen, letting down her hair, and fluffing the curly mass into a casual, loose shape. Her glance at the wall phone showed that she had one message. This was her personal phone, not the office line downstairs.

Picking up the receiver, she pressed the message button.

"Hi, Holly. This is Nick Conway. It's seven p.m. here and I'm done for the day at my mother's diner. I'd like to talk to you about that apartment you have available. I forgot to ask you if you'd allow Snowflake, my dog, to live there with me. Could you give me a call and we'll sort this all out?"

Holly quickly wrote down his number on a magnetic pad that hung next to the phone. She tried not to be affected by his mellow voice, but she was. Looking at her watch, she saw it was nearly 7:30 in the evening. Should she call him now?

Her heart made the decision for her and she resolutely picked up the phone. Her palms became damp as the phone rang several times before it was answered.

"Nick? This is Holly. I'm returning your call from earlier." She sounded a little breathless, her fingers tightening a bit around the phone.

"Hi, Holly. I guess I didn't expect to hear from you tonight."

Every part of her body relaxed beneath his low voice. She could now see why he was a dog handler. It was as if nothing got under his skin. "No, I just got done feeding my shut-ins and saw there was a message on my phone. Are you still interested in that corner apartment?"

"Yes, I think I am. But it depends upon two things. First, Snowflake has to be allowed to live with me. And if that's okay with you, then I need to know how much the rent is a month."

"I think every one of my tenants has a cat or dog," she said, "so Snowflake won't be an issue at all. I find people actually calm down and their blood pressure lowers when they live with an animal."

"Oh, good."

She heard the relief in his voice and added, "We talked a little about how I do a trade for services so tenants don't have to pay as much for monthly rent."

"Yes, you mentioned that."

"As it happens, Oscar Duarte, my driver, passed away two weeks ago and I desperately need someone who could drive me around and help me deliver the food to my ten shut-ins after I prepare the food here. It's seven days a week," she said. "Would you be interested in that kind of a job?"

He was silent, mulling it over, then said, "Yes, I think I could handle that. How much would the rent be?"

"Well, the rent on that apartment is a hundred dollars a month. Delos gives me a yearly budget and I was paying Oscar ten dollars an hour. I could pay you twice a month. Your check may vary because my shut-ins sometimes need more attention, or I have to go back so we can take them to the doctor, the hospital, the eye doctor, the dentist, or to the town's orthopedic clinic, for example."

She was talking nonstop now, and she always got that way when she was nervous. Taking a deep breath, Holly added, "Do you think you could do a trade, Nick? Would that suit you?" Holly held her breath never wanting more than for him to say, "Yes."

"I'm signed up for a computer science degree here at the local community college. It's a two-year degree. I'm taking classes, but some of them I can get downloaded onto my computer. The rest, I have to be there in person."

"Of course," she murmured. "I understand."

"The government is paying for my college degree, which is a godsend for me under the circumstances. And I could use a part-time job like you're offering me."

Her heart did a flip. "Oh, great! I'm so excited, Nick! Thank you so much for doing this! Would you like to come over and see the apartment tonight? You and Snowflake? See if he likes it, too?"

Holly knew how excited she got and she was probably scaring off the guy. Nick seemed so quiet, reticent, and thoughtful. He probably thought she was a yo-yo without a string to pull her back together. She grinned, unable to stop the joy from bubbling up through her.

"Sure, I know where you're located. It will take me about fifteen minutes. See you then."

Holly felt a magical, invisible connection between them and sensed his sudden happiness; she could hear how his tone lightened. A thrill raced through her. She knew he would be a hard, responsible worker because his mother had told her, and she knew military people much better than anyone ever realized, even Sue. Holly understood the hope she heard in Nick's voice— it was as if she were throwing him a life preserver in that roiling, black sea of feelings that constantly tossed him around.

CHAPTER 2

HOLLY SAW THE headlights of a car turn into the parking area next to the Delos Charity building. From her apartment at the end of the building, she had a full view of the area. A few minutes later, the low-wattage street lamps revealed Nick Conway and Snowflake approaching the building. Snowflake was on a six-foot leash. He was panting and looked happy. Her gaze moved to Nick, who was hunched over in a black, nylon winter coat that fell just below his hips. He wore a black baseball cap on his short hair and she was sure his ears were freezing. The man wasn't wearing a muffler or gloves, either. She knew how cold Afghanistan could become and his body was probably still acclimated to that harsh, cold weather, instead of the milder winters they were accustomed to in this part of Montana. But then again, Montana winters could also be pretty brutal.

Holly noticed Nick looking around, ever alert. She knew it was a natural reaction for a WMD handler out at the front of his platoon, although he was no longer in that level of danger. It was Nick's responsibility to keep the men behind him safe. Holly wasn't sure she could ever do that kind of job because the danger was constant. Both man and dog looked very alert, as if they were still living in a war-torn country. But the dog was more well-adjusted than his owner, that was for sure. She struggled with memories that could overwhelm her if she allowed. Holly had had enough grief over the last three years, always hoping the intensity of that gut-wrenching feeling would eventually wear off. Somehow, it never seemed to lose its ferocity, much to her chagrin.

The look in Nick Conway's eyes earlier today was identical to the one she remembered in her older sister, Noelle's, eyes: flat and disengaged from life. She realized with a pang just how much she missed her larger-than-life sister. Often, Holly thought of Noelle, knowing that she no longer suffered pain and anguish. She was finally at peace. Finally.

Worriedly, she watched Nick and Snowflake make their way across the mostly dry parking lot. Now, she watched Nick avoid the few remaining slick ice patches illuminated by the lights above.

So did Snowflake, who was delicately moving around such isolated spots to keep his beloved handler safe from slipping.

The fact that Nick's gaze looked a lot like Noelle's made her heart tug with concern. He appeared to be very nice, more aware than other men she'd met in her life. Being a WMD handler, Holly thought, as she stepped out the front door to greet them, such sensitivity was necessary. Dogs don't speak English. A handler had to have a very keen eye, and strong intuition, linked with the ability, in her opinion, to communicate with a dog hunting for explosives. She knew that the same kind of sensitivity could create deep, ongoing wounds within Nick, too, and she was sure he had them. She would bet Snowflake did, too.

"Hey, Nick!" she called from the black, wrought-iron balcony on the second floor, waving down at him, "Take the side steps over there and come on up!" she said, pointing to her right.

He halted at her greeting, his face lifting up toward hers, and for a moment, he smiled, really smiled, and waved. Snowflake tugged hard on the leash, seeming to understand what she had just said, wanting to go toward that staircase at the end of the building she'd pointed to. "Thanks," he called. "Be right up."

Holly wrapped her arms around herself,

shivering—the temperature was in the twenties already. She had to smile as she watched Snowflake leap against his leash, tugging Nick along. Did Snowflake understand English? Moving back into her warm apartment, she waited near the door, keeping her eye on the window next to it, waiting for the duo to appear.

When they arrived at the door, she said, "Hi! Come on in." There was a big, thick brown rug in the foyer, and a wooden bench along the wall where a person could sit down and trade their wet boots for a dry pair. His boots were dry, so he just wiped them off good on the bristly rug.

"Aren't you cold without a muffler, hat, and gloves?" she asked incredulously. Leaning down, she petted Snowflake. The dog's short, bobbed tail gleefully wriggled his entire hind end, and his blue eyes gazed at her adoringly. She laughed with delight, smoothing the white, gray, and black fur over his head and neck.

Nick stomped his feet once more on the rug. "My mother lectures me about that, too," he admitted, grinning over at her.

"Sue is practical, just like me," Holly laughed. She stepped to the door to show him to his apartment, and he noticed that she wasn't wearing a coat.

"Hey," he said, stepping aside to allow her to pass. "Don't you need a coat?"

"Do as I say, not as I do?" she teased him

unmercifully. She saw redness rush up into his cheeks and it was touching.

"Caught red-handed," he grumped good naturedly.

Pleased with his concern for her, she said, "No, it's a quick trip down the passageway here. Follow me, okay?" The stars were glimmering in the night. Her breath shot out in white wisps as she hurriedly led them down the covered area. Slipping the key into the lock, she opened the door and then flipped on the lights.

"Go on in," she invited.

"No, ladies first," he demurred, gesturing for Holly to move ahead of him. Snowflake sat obediently at his side, watching her with interest.

"That's what I love about military folks," she said, stepping onto a thick, black rug.

"What's that?"

"You're so gentlemanly in a day and age when it seems like it's been lost."

"I guess we are, in some ways," he said, stepping in and closing the door. "Years of training, first by my parents, then reinforced by the military, you know . . ."

"Well, I appreciate it," she told him, turning. "This is a two-bedroom unit. It's just a bit smaller than my apartment. The big units are up on the second floor. Come on in, and welcome home!"

★

NICK TRIED TO ignore Holly's closeness, but her sweet, feminine scent, or perhaps the shampoo she used on her glorious red hair, was extremely pleasant, and he breathed it in like a life-affirming elixir. Right now, he was aware that life here was a far cry from his life in Afghanistan.

He leaned down and removed Snowflake's leash, knowing his dog would remain obediently at his side. Holly's swaying hips as she led him through the room reminded him how long it had been since he'd made love to a woman. It seemed like another lifetime.

Only Snowflake grounded him, reminding him of reality, and brought out the natural caring he had for living things, whether animals or people. This was just one of the many ways his dog had become his lifesaver.

Nick followed Holly into an open-concept living room and kitchen. "Nice," he said, because he knew she wanted feedback.

"Let's go to the kitchen," she said eagerly.

Nick stood next to her, not so close as to crowd her, but silently enjoying her nearness. Her casual, gray gym outfit somehow looked fetching, even sexy, on Holly. He liked that she wasn't self-conscious. That ruffling of red hair around her shoulders made her oval, freckled face something he wanted to study and remember even more than before. She was actually becoming beautiful to him.

"This," he said awkwardly, "looks fine, too."

"Do you cook much?" she asked.

"My mom insisted I learn how to cook, so yes, I won't starve."

Holly laughed and his heart responded with a flow of warmth cascading through him. Her eyes brimmed with such life that he ached to feel that way himself.

"Great. Are you happy with the living room?" she asked.

In Nick's eyes, it was absolutely sumptuous, with a dark green, corduroy sofa and two overstuffed chairs arranged around a huge, square wooden coffee table with a glass top. "Yeah, looks fine. Much nicer than what I'm used to, believe me."

"Your military life will always follow you around, more or less, won't it?" she posed softly, giving him an understanding look.

His mouth thinned for a moment, and he didn't answer. Then he asked, "How about the bedrooms? What do they look like?" Nick couldn't go into his military life with her, although he wanted to. He sensed that Holly was the kind of person who could hold him and heal him. He didn't know why he knew that—it was just what his heart whispered to him. For so long, it had felt frozen and numb. Until right now.

"Sure," she said. "This way."

He liked following Holly. She had such energy and enthusiasm that he couldn't resist being close to her.

"This is the master bedroom, so to speak," she said wryly, stepping in and gesturing to a queen-size bed, an oak antique dresser, and a chair in one corner. "I know it's not much . . ."

"Are you kidding me?" Nick looked around. "It's more than I ever expected. Did you decorate this place?"

"Sort of. Dilara Culver, who owns Delos Charities, had a designer fly in and look at the blueprints for this building so it no longer looked like a motel. She brought all kinds of furniture catalogs with her that I could choose from. Together, I think we did a pretty good job."

Nodding as he looked around, Nick spotted the bathroom off the main room. "You did. I like those dark-green velvety drapes. It will keep the cold from the window from leaking into the room."

"They're velour, and that's why I chose them. The windows are double-paned to prevent heat loss and keep out that bitter winter cold."

"I like Dilara Culver's attitude," he murmured appreciatively. Nick knew double-paned windows cost twice as much as a single-paned one, but they were worth every extra cent. A small shelf held books supported by bookends of wranglers riding bronzed bucking broncos. He was now back in the Old West and he'd always liked furniture from that era.

"Dilara is incredible, a dream come true," Holly agreed. "Your master bathroom is over there. It has a bathtub and shower. This apartment comes furnished with everything, so all you have to do is move in your stuff and you're good to go."

"Well, that works for me, since I didn't bring much back from Afghanistan."

"Probably just an Army duffle bag?" she guessed, glancing up at him.

"Yep. You seem to know a lot about the military," he added observantly.

Shrugging, she said, "My dad was in the Marine Corps for twenty years."

"So, Holly, are you a military brat who was moved from one base to another every two years?"

"Sort of," she admitted. "My dad was deployed a lot to Iraq, so we stayed at Camp Pendleton in southern California." Holly turned and gestured across the hall. "You might want to use this room as an office or a workout room. It has lots of possibilities."

Following her, he saw it was already set up as an office. "Sure," he said. "I like that antique oak roll-top desk. Where did you find that?"

"Right here in Hamilton at Candy's Antique Store at the other end of town."

"Nice to see you tried to work with local

businesses so they got part of the money in this rebuild."

"Dilara always tries to involve local contractors and businesses when she has a Delos charity built in their town. About half the antiques in this two-story building come from Candy's shop. She was tickled pink about it."

"She always had nice antiques," Nick told her. "As a kid I used to run down the wooden sidewalk from our diner to her store. I always liked nosing around and she was nice about answering my questions."

"Candy's in her seventies now, and I think she's probably going to try and sell her store because it's just getting to be too much for her," Holly said, concern in her tone. "Her husband, Steve, died two years ago and it devastated her. I feel so deeply for her. They had thirty-five years together, and they had a happy marriage, like your folks do."

"I didn't know about Candy's husband," he offered, frowning. "I've only been back for two weeks and I'm trying to get my life under control. My mom knows all the local gossip, but we haven't had time to sit down and talk about the people who have lived here all their lives. I'm sorry Steve is gone, he was a good man."

"You know how small Hamilton is. Everyone knows everyone else. Most of the people were born here and live their whole lives here.

When someone passes, the whole town grieves."

"I remember attending more than a few funerals while growing up here," he said. "Tell me more about yourself. When did you come to Hamilton? It must have been while I was in the Army."

"Tell you what," she said, "let's close the deal on this apartment and then we can celebrate by letting me make you a cup of hot chocolate back at my place. I'll tell you more, then?"

He couldn't have asked for a better celebration—this woman was one bundle of good ideas! "Yeah, I'll take the place. It's much better than I'd expected, and at only a hundred dollars a month . . . are you sure?" He saw the sparkle come to her eyes, her full lips crooked into a grin.

"Only if you agree to be my van driver when you can. I know you have college and classes you have to attend. On those days or times, I can drive the van myself like I'm doing right now."

He held out his hand toward her, wanting to feel her soft one against the hard, calloused quality of his own. "You've got a deal, Holly. Thanks for offering me and Snowflake this apartment, plus that part-time job."

Shaking his hand, she grinned and released it. "Here are your keys. You can stay here tonight, if you want."

"I'd like to, but I can't. I'm driving my mom and dad nuts at their place and I'm sure they'll be glad to hear I've got an apartment near them."

She laughed a little. "I understand. Okay, do you need any help with your duffle bag or anything else? I can help you carry in whatever you have in your car."

"No, that's okay. Everything is over at my parents' home. I'll bring the stuff over with me tomorrow."

"Great. Come on. We deserve some exceptionally wonderful hot chocolate, and I have a secret recipe I think you'll love!"

Snowflake whined, his tail-stub and butt wriggling as Holly passed near them, heading out to the hall.

Nick felt lighter. Happier. He would be living right next door to Holly. She wore no ring on her hand to indicate she was married or going with someone. Nick just couldn't believe she didn't have a man in her life, though. "Okay, lead the way," he told her.

HOLLY WATCHED NICK'S face change as he sipped the hot chocolate. There was no doubt that he was the latest convert to Holly's secret family recipe. He'd already swiped the thick, whipped cream from his mug onto his finger and given it to a very appreciative Snowflake.

Holly smiled. "I think Snowflake worships

you," she said, sitting at his elbow at the square, wooden table in her kitchen. She'd set out some leftover cookies from today's run that had been made by her other helper, Janie Le Baron. Nick said little, but gratitude was written on his features as he sipped the chocolate and eagerly consumed three of the six cookies.

She noticed that, unlike other guys, Nick was unselfishly leaving half the cookies for her to eat—another promising quality on her dream partner's list. Nick seemed to be the whole package, but she cautioned herself.

"Tell me about when you moved to Hamilton," he said to her.

"I came here after graduating from college in Missoula, Montana, at age twenty-two. I received a degree in social work."

"Were either of your parents in that line of work?" he wondered.

Shaking her head, she said, "After my dad retired from the Corps, he created his own construction company up in Missoula. Mom was a day care helper. It was a job she could easily continue if Dad was sent off to another base."

"She must have loved kids," he observed, wondering if Holly took after her mom.

Giving him a soft look, Holly whispered, "Yes, it's definitely in my genes! I can remember taking care of children wherever we were stationed. I'd get home from school and help her with the kids in the late afternoons and evenings."

"Like mother, like daughter," Nick said. He saw Snowflake get up and move over next to Holly, lying his head on her thigh, offering an adoring look as he gazed up at her. "Do you want me to call him back?" he asked. Holly seemed to like Snowflake, but you never could be sure about people.

Placing her hand on Snowflake's broad head, she smiled a little. "No, I love dogs and cats. I'd have one myself, but I'm so busy I couldn't be home to let them out or to get much exercise. That wouldn't be fair to them."

Nodding, he watched Holly's features grow tender as she gently ran her hand from Snowflake's head down his spotted grey and black back. "Even though he was trained by the Army to find bombs and explosives, my dog always knew when one of the guys needed a little love. He'd always go over and do what he's doing with you."

Holly felt her secret heartache and whispered, "Snowflake senses things . . . things I usually don't tell anyone." Giving the shepherd a kind look, she lifted her chin, finding comfort in Nick's interested expression. Dog and owner, she realized, were mirrors of one another. That gave her the courage to go on. Her hand stilled on Snowflake's shoulders as he sat there, his head resting on her thigh like a warm blanket.

"I had an older sister, Noelle, who was three years older than me. She was born on Christmas Eve. I was born on Christmas Day three years later. That's why we got Christmas names," she said, smiling fondly, seeing Nick's eyes grow warm with understanding. "Noelle followed in my dad's footsteps and joined the Navy when she was eighteen. She became a medical corpsman. I went another direction because I knew I didn't have what it took to be in the military."

She moved her fingers slowly through Snowflake's silky fur. "I'd just graduated college when, a couple of weeks later, my parents were both killed in a car accident."

Nick winced. "That must have been terrible for you both."

"It was. And it seemed like nothing but bad luck followed me and my sister that year. When Noelle came home from Iraq for the funeral, I was absolutely terrified of her.

"In what way?"

Nick's voice held out such comfort, she allowed herself to continue.

"She had PTSD. She was a Navy corpsman attached to a Marine company and was often at fire bases near the enemy. One day, she was tending Marines along with the doctor who came with her, and the base was nearly overrun by an assault of enemy soldiers. She thought they would all be killed, but at the last moment, our A-10 Warthogs arrived and drove back the enemy."

She took a small sip of her chocolate. "When Noelle came home for the funeral, I saw deadness in her eyes for the first time. I felt as if I didn't even know who she was. She was closed up, hard, and deeply depressed."

Reaching over, Nick covered her hand for a moment. "That comes from being in too many firefights, Holly. Seeing things no one should ever see. They stay with you, unfortunately. They never leave." He waited a moment, then pulled his hand reluctantly away from hers.

"I was too grief-stricken to realize it at the time. I was bawling my eyes out at the funeral, but Noelle just sat there like a robot, unfeeling. I couldn't believe it. I didn't understand what had happened to her." She swallowed hard and held his gaze. "I tried to talk to her, find out why, but she got angry at me and told me I'd never understand. She told me to leave her alone."

Holly pushed her hands against her face for a moment, "And it devastated me. We'd been so close growing up. I was always the little sister tagging along after her. And after the funeral, she went to a local bar in Missoula and got drunk. She never drank before leaving for the Navy, Nick." Snowflake leaned up, licking her closest hand, now limp on her lap, repeatedly with his pink tongue. She gave the dog a grateful look and scratched behind his ears.

"PTSD will do that to you." Nick sighed heavily, "It will make you depressed and numb, Holly. You don't feel any of your emotions except for anxiety. And a lot of men and women in the military have PTSD. There are two ways to dull that anxiety: take prescription drugs or drink. It sounds like Noelle chose alcohol as a way to bury her anxiety."

"You have PTSD, too, don't you Nick?"

Mouth tightening, he nodded. "Yeah. Snowflake and I saw too much, like so many others. There are things I wish I could forget, but I know I never will." He pulled his wallet from his back pocket. "Here, I want to show you something. I don't know if this will make you feel any better . . ." He pulled a frayed photo from his wallet and slid it in front of her. "This was Dude, a yellow Labrador, my first WMD dog."

She picked up the photo that was partially torn from a lot of handling over a long time. Holly studied the photo. Nick was in his Army Corps combat gear, a floppy, desert camouflage hat on his head, with Dude sitting next to him in his harness, panting. Nick was smiling, and so was Dude. "You two look so close," she whispered, holding the photo gently between her hands. "Like you belong together. I love this photo so much because Dude is actually smiling. Look at his lower teeth exposed! That's amazing!"

"Yeah," he rasped, "you're right, he would smile like that when he was trying to lift my spirits or when we were happy doing something together. I got him assigned to me when I was nineteen and I had him until I was twenty-three."

"What happened to him, Nick?" Holly searched his anguished eyes.

Snowflake whined, got up, and went back to his master's right side, lying his head on Nick's thigh. Automatically, Nick's hand came to rest on his head, as if needing the dog's love and reassurance.

"Dude was following down a scent inside a walled Afghan village," he said, his voice laced with pain. "I had him on a sixteen-foot leash and there was a door torn off this mud and rock hut of a barn where goats were kept. He went in there, following the scent and disappeared. The next thing I knew, I felt this blast of heat and a pressure wave throwing me backward, off my feet. I remember not being able to hear because both my eardrums were blown out in the blast. Some of my team later told me I tumbled end over end for at least six feet before I hit the wall around the village. They found me unconscious."

Fingers against her lips, her eyes huge, Holly whispered, "Oh, no! Poor, beautiful Dude . . . and you . . . you could have died, too, Nick!"

CHAPTER 3

"DUDE SAVED MY life so many times," Nick choked out, his voice a hoarse whisper. When Holly slid the photo gently back into his hand, he hungrily absorbed that momentary touch of her fingers. "He was my first dog, and he was this incredible human being in an animal's body." Giving Snowflake a loving look, Nick patted him. "I gave up living after Dude was killed. I was not only wounded, I was messed up inside, as well. It's hard to explain how close we had been and I was grieving for the fact that I'd never see him smile at me like that again."

Holly shook her head. "Hey, it's not hard to understand how much you two shared. He kept you and the other guys safe for so many years. You slept with him, you fed him, and you cared for him. Not only was he your protector, you were his," she posed quietly.

Nick felt a twisting, gut-wrenching grief reawaken in his heart. "You're right, Holly, Dude was all those things to me, and more. He kept me sane. There were times when I felt I was part of a computer war game looking at the carnage after a firefight. I just couldn't take it all in. No one could."

"Noelle once told me that I couldn't understand the terror, the constant threats to her and those she worked with over in Iraq. She felt lost, sometimes, with nothing to hold on to, nothing to make her remember the good things about our life before she served. She saw so much suffering every day over there." Tilting her head, Holly held his devastated gaze, Dude's photo resting in his palm. "Did Dude remind you of the kinder, more positive aspects of life?"

Giving her a careful look, Nick cleared his throat and rasped, "You're pretty insightful, but then again, I knew you would be. Yeah, Dude kept my humanity, my sanity, and reminded me of a different, better time before I deployed. I couldn't believe how those people lived over there in Afghanistan. They were always on the edge of survival and starvation. There was no guarantee that they'd have a crop of grain grow and mature so that their family wouldn't starve the next winter. Or that their fruit trees would have a big crop instead of a little one." He shook his head, "I just never realized until I got over there, how little the Afghan people had. Every day was a Herculean effort to survive. It was a heartbreaking place to be, Holly."

"And Dude helped you get through every day?"

"Very much so. At night, when we were back behind the wire, we had a corner in a room with some pieces of cardboard to sleep on, plus a couple of blankets. But it was Dude who kept me warm. He was alive, loving, licking me, always playful, and he made me laugh when I wanted to cry. There were days that were horrifying for me, Holly. Death lives right next to you all the time. On some nights I was so damned tired, my speech was slurred. I'd just lie down, wanting desperately to sleep because I was physically worn out."

"I don't think people realize how much our dogs and cats give to us. It was probably even more brutal on you when it got cold over there."

"Winters were always cold over there and our rooms weren't heated. Dude was a short-haired dog, but his coat got thicker for the winter. He'd crawl right up to me, put his head on my shoulder, press his big, long eighty-pound body alongside mine and sleep. He kept me warm. He made me feel safe when I knew there was no safety anywhere in that godforsaken country. And if I had to cry, I'd just bury my face into his fur and let it all out. He never moved then, he knew I needed to cry. Then, I'd finally be able to sleep."

"Dude was special," she agreed. Her voice turned gentle, "Did you receive any other wounds from that blast at the Afghan barn?"

Shrugging, he said, "Mostly shrapnel, rocks, and mud hitting me full on. I had a Kevlar vest on, but my face, neck, arms, and legs took the brunt of it." He touched a small white scar along the left side of his jaw. "A rock got me there. I remember becoming conscious on the Medevac flight back to Bagram. I had a lot of facial cuts, minor bleeding, but no severe wounds. When we got to the hospital at Bagram, the doc told me later I'd had a hundred stitches total on my body. I stayed there for two days and then they released me back to my unit."

"That wasn't long enough to heal," Holly noted grimly. "Did they give you any counseling to help with Dude's loss?"

He gave her a wry look. "No, but I got sent back to the States after my CO took one look at me." Giving Snowflake a tender look, he added, "The Corps wanted to hook me up with another WMD dog right away and get me redeployed."

"Wow! That had to twist you up," Holly said. "They weren't giving you time to adjust, breathe, or move through your grief over losing Dude."

"That's the military, Holly. They needed WMD handlers and dogs more than anything else over there. IEDs were everywhere, all the time.

The military was much more interested in saving a lot of American lives than worrying about how well I was handling Dude's loss. I understand and I don't blame anyone for the situation. I wanted to save American lives, too."

Shaking her head, she whispered unsteadily, "Well, I'd need time to come down from the shock of being blown off my feet and work through my loss of Dude. I guess I don't have that kind of emotional toughness." Her lips thinned for a moment. "Noelle told me once that I was like a clam without a shell, and that anyone going into the military had to have that shell in place to survive everything they experienced over there."

"I guess I'm not good at having that shell, either," Nick admitted, continuing to stroke Snowflake's head. His dog was looking up at him, blue eyes filled with concern. He knew his dog felt his every emotion and this time, he didn't try to hide it. "I tried, but it never worked well. Dude was my shell. When he'd snuggle into my arms and we'd sleep together, I felt like things would be all right. I knew he was there to protect me if it came to that."

Holly gazed warmly at Snowflake. "Tell me how Snowflake has helped you. I'm sure he has—he's so loving!"

Nick nodded, scratching Snowflake's black ear. "When I got sent back to the training school stateside, they assigned me to this guy. I was angry, hurting, grieving, and depressed. I didn't want to take Snowflake," and he gave his dog a sad look of apology.

"I've never heard of Australian shepherds being used as WMD dogs," Holly said.

"They use all kinds of breeds. Dogs with longer noses have a better sniffer," Nick told her.

"How did he get his name?" Holly smiled a little, watching the shepherd respond to their interest in him.

"When he was a puppy, his flanks had a lot of gray with black spots over it." Nick moved his hand across Snowflake's back. "The breeder's little daughter named him."

"The name fits him," Holly agreed. "He's so smart and alert."

"Well, herding dogs are like that, although I was told by the instructors that Snowflake was the smartest of all their dogs in training at that time. He's super athletic and was used to herding sheep. So, in our case, he saw me and our Army company as his sheep band to protect," Nick said, managing a small smile. "He must have felt the emotional shape I was in because he was very affectionate, always had his body against my leg unless he was hunting for IEDs. A dog can sense all your emotions. And when I took him back after training was over, to Afghanistan, I think he considered me his number one priority."

"Even though he hunted for IEDs every day?"

"Yeah," Nick said, ruffling Snowflake's fur along his neck, "In some ways, he reminded me of Dude. Both had that nurturing instinct."

"You slept together like you did with Dude?"

"Yes. I always had a feeling that Snowflake knew how dangerous his work was. He was far more athletic and aggressive than Dude ever was. It was as if he understood in his dog's mind that he was responsible for all of us. But that's the herd dog's genes at work, too. A Lab isn't a herd dog, although they have one of the best noses in the business, which is why they're used so much on deployments."

"Well," Holly said, smiling down at Snowflake, "he's a very special dog." She lifted her chin, meeting, and holding Nick's gaze.

"He's all of that and more," he agreed.

"And so are you."

"No," Nick protested, "I'm nothing special, believe me. I'm just a survivor, that's all."

"Well," Holly said pertly, drinking the last of her hot chocolate, "you're special to me."

Those words sent a burst of warmth to his heart, threading the first strands of hope through him to have some kind of normal life once again. "I'm just trying to survive, Holly, that's all. I'm trying to get my new life under me and get into some kind of fixed routine that will allow me to adjust to civilian ways of living. I'm hoping the shadows of Afghanistan will start to fade away."

"I know," she whispered gently. Then, changing the subject, "So when would you like to go to work as my van driver?"

"How about the day after tomorrow? I need to move my duffle from my parents' home to here, and I have a three-hour class tomorrow afternoon learning to write software code."

"Sounds good," she said. "Would you mind bringing Snowflake along? My shut-ins love dogs and cats, even though they don't have any. Can a WMD dog tolerate being petted by a bunch of strangers?"

"Sure. Snowflake loves people. Anyone he meets, he automatically adds to his doggie list of dependents." Nick found he was drowning in Holly's soft gaze. She represented so much of what he'd lost over in Afghanistan. Just sitting here with her had tamped down most of his anxiety.

Holly fed him far more than hot chocolate. She gave him a sense of belonging, a sense of peace, and a feeling of acceptance. Nick wanted to ask her so many personal questions, but he didn't. He'd seen photos of her with her parents and her sister, Noelle, on her desk. He didn't see any photos that showed her with a special man in her life.

Was it crazy to wish that he could be that

special person? What could he give her except sleepless nights when he awoke screaming from the nightmares and flashbacks he still had? Yet, his foolish heart murmured that he had a chance with Holly. To Nick, it felt like a dream that could never come true.

WHERE HAD THE last six weeks flown? Holly laughed as she placed a small pumpkin that she and Nick had carved a funny face into, inside the van. Tomorrow was Halloween and he had suggested a week earlier that they buy some small pumpkins, carve faces in them, and give the pumpkins to their ten elders. It was a great idea!

She'd grown so used to Nick driving the van and helping her carry in the dinners to her elders, that she wondered what her life would be like without Nick in it. Never mind that Snowflake was deeply loved and eagerly welcomed by all her clients. How they looked forward to the shepherd bounding into their homes, his stub going a million miles an hour, eagerly licking their paper-thin hands. The dog always brought laughter and smiles, and that was important to Holly.

She knew how depressed older people could become. Many of the loved ones that had once inhabited their lives were now dead and gone. Their families might be a whole coast away, unable to take them in and care for them. So they lived alone, with just a radio and TV to keep them company.

Nick, after he'd seen the situation with her shut-ins, had suggested that he bring Snowflake around for a half hour or so visit with each elder, once a week. She loved that he put himself out to others like that. Snowflake, of course, enjoyed being idolized, and all the elders were better off because of their volunteer work. As for Nick, his participation was bringing him out of a deep, dark well, slowly returning him to life.

Having invited Nick and Snowflake to her apartment for Halloween dinner, Holly had warned him that the local kids would arrive at her door in droves. She had been concerned that the laughter of children, their high energy, and excited voices might put him on edge. Of course, she had asked him and he was fine with it.

Never did Nick make a move to flirt with her. He was always a gentleman, opening a door for her, walking on the outside of the sidewalk with her on the inside. He always put her first, and she was more than grateful for his sensitivity and care of her. And it was care.

But Holly wanted more from Nick. Much more.

Halloween night was not the right time or place to learn more about him. Despite his friendly approach to her, Nick was a deeply private person. Unless she asked the right question, he didn't volunteer anything about himself. And sometimes, Holly wondered if he felt she was nosy because she was always asking him questions. But how else was she to get to know him on more than just a casual basis?

NICK MADE SURE before meeting Holly for Halloween evening that he took a quick shower and pulled on a bright, orange sweatshirt along with a pair of black, chino pants. He smiled to himself, he'd look like a proverbial pumpkin tonight for the kids. Snowflake sat in the entrance of the bathroom, watching him like he always did. He quickly pulled a comb through his short hair. "Okay, let's get dessert," he told Snowflake. The dog got up, wagging his stub.

Nick thought a pumpkin pie was in keeping for tonight. It was already dark at six p.m. and at least twenty kids and their attending parents had come to his apartment door. He had a huge bowl of candy, fresh fruit, and other goodies sitting on the small desk in the foyer.

His heart felt lighter. Even though he was sure their dinner would be interrupted and that serious conversations were out of the question, he still looked forward to tonight. Picking up the pumpkin pie, he told Snowflake to follow him, and as he looked out the door, he saw no kids approaching. Yet. Grinning, he remembered how much he had looked forward to Halloween as a child.

Hurrying down the covered passageway, he was gently pelted by slow, fat snowflakes. The moon was nearly full, lending a beautiful radiance between the sulfur lights of the parking lot below, and the lights in town, when the clouds parted for a moment. He heard kids giggling below and hurried to Holly's door, knocking on it.

"Hey, come in," she called, smiling and standing aside.

That honeysuckle scent, Nick had found out, was the shampoo she used. Tonight, that red, curly mass was gleaming around her face, emphasizing her large, blue eyes. She was beautiful, freckles and all. And the soft-pink angora sweater she wore along with black, wool slacks emphasized it. "There's a bunch of kids down below," he warned with a grin, stepping inside.

"Oh," Holly said, "I'm sure. What do you have for our dessert?" she asked, craning her neck, looking up at the pie he held in his hands.

"Pumpkin?"

Her lips drew away from her teeth. "I have whipped cream."

"Oh," Nick teased, giving Snowflake an important look, "he'll like that, too."

"That," she said, turning and walking with him into the kitchen, "is because he's a whipped cream aficionado and you feed his habit, Conway." They walked down the hall, laughing.

Nick absorbed the lilt of her laughter as he placed the pie on the kitchen counter. "Guilty as charged. Smells good. What did you make?"

"Well, you said you're a meat-and-potatoes kind of guy, so I slow cooked a roast, potatoes, celery, and carrots." She moved over to the stove. "I'm in the process of making a nice, dark-brown gravy to go with it."

How badly Nick wanted to lift his fingers and move that copper hair aside and kiss the slender nape of her neck. What would Holly do if he did something like that? Nick entertained those kinds of thoughts every day he was with her. It was damned tough to keep his hands to himself, to keep his conversations social, not serious or soul-searching. Holly was a complex person. He wanted to know how she saw the world, what she was thinking, and so much more.

While Holly was making the fragrant gravy, the doorbell rang.

"Your turn," Holly called over her shoulder.

"Yep," he murmured. Opening the door, Snowflake sat at his side, wriggling his stub. There were two parents, both women, with four children between them. Nick smiled as he put a fresh apple, along with a small candy bar, into each sack. Two of the children came forward to eagerly, spontaneously pet Snowflake. Nick assured the mothers that he wouldn't bite, so they let their kids pet him.

As he closed the door, he said, "The kids are just as taken with Snowflake as they are with getting the candy."

Holly poured the finished gravy into a bowl. "I'm not surprised. Snowflake has such a kind face." She rinsed out her pan in the sink and then added, "Like his master."

Wandering into the warm kitchen filled with all kinds of delicious fragrances, Nick took the bowl of gravy and added a spoon to it from the drawer. "I've never had a woman tell me I had a kind face before."

Giving him a teasing glance as she rinsed off her hands and dried them on a nearby towel, Holly said, "That was a compliment, by the way."

"Thanks," he said, placing the bowl on a metal trivet. Holly had already placed white plates with red roses around them on the table. In many ways, she was very old fashioned, loving antiques and anything from the 1900s. There was no new furniture in her home except for the couch and two matching, overstuffed chairs. Everything else, he'd learned, had come from Candy's antique store as she saved for the particular piece she wanted to buy.

"Ready to eat?" she asked, coming over to

the table.

Nick pulled out the chair for her. "More than ready. Smells great, Holly."

She gave him a look of thanks and sat down.

In short order, he had a plate filled with steaming mashed potatoes slathered in gravy, two thick slices of beef roast, and several heaping spoonsful of carrots and celery. "You're a much better cook than I am," he admitted, smiling into her eyes as she ate daintily.

Snowflake whined, sitting at his right side, looking up and watching as Nick enjoyed his meal.

"Thanks. I love to cook. I don't get a lot of personal time, as you know, to do that. But when I can get a few uninterrupted hours, I like to make something good to eat."

Nick knew that she often made salads, tuna fish, or other quick-to-fix foods because of her schedule. "Have you thought of getting a manager in here to help you?"

Shrugging, she licked her lips and then patted them with her paper napkin. "Yes and no. I've been doing this ever since I graduated from college. Guess I'm a horse in a harness and I have a fixed routine that works for me, Nick."

"But it doesn't give you any downtime for yourself."

"Oh," she grimaced, "that . . ."

He knew it was a point of contention with

Holly. "I'm pretty good at basic accounting. I might be able to take that over for you. It would free you up a lot, Holly. I see you laboring in your office with those accounting books."

"Numbers aren't my thing," she admitted, scowling. "I mean, I can do it. It's just no fun, is all."

"Numbers is something that come easy to me. Would you like me to maybe help you out a little?"

"But you're so busy yourself, Nick!" She gave him an exasperated look. "Talk about the pot calling the kettle black! You run from a class back here, help me load up the dinners, and we're off. You don't stop until we get back here, and then you have a lot of studying and homework assignments to do." She shook a finger at him. "I've seen a light on in your apartment until three a.m. some mornings."

"Caught," he said, chuckling. "I'm learning to write code. It takes time. But I'm getting better at it and I have an affinity for it. I don't mind the late hours."

"But you're not getting the sleep you need."

He warmed to her concern. "My mom told me the other day when I dropped in to see her, that because I'm in my twenties, I can burn the candle at both ends and get away with it. And if I have to do that, Holly, I will. A two-year degree in computer science will support me the rest of my life. We're already getting contacted by Apple people. They're looking to hire us after the first year."

"Really?"

"Yeah," he said, "that's kinda nice. And their pay is good."

"Well," she said, "will that mean you have to move to Silicon Valley?"

He saw something in her blue eyes that moved him—tension, maybe? "No, I talked to their rep about it and she said that often things can be handled long-distance and there's no move involved."

"Do you want to move? I mean, you just got home, Nick."

There was something else going on here and he couldn't figure it out. "I have a choice to make, but I know my mom needs help. I was born here and I like the town and its people. I've been gone because of my military service and I don't think my mother would be happy if I left a year from now."

"Oh, good," she whispered, relief in her voice, "I'm glad. I want you to stay, too, Nick."

His heart stirred. There was such sincerity in her voice and in her eyes that he almost reached out to graze her pink cheek.

"I could still help you out, Holly." He saw her become flustered, as if she wanted to say more to him, but just then, the doorbell rang.

"My turn," she said, getting up, and putting the paper napkin beside her plate.

Snowflake quickly got up, following Holly to the door. He sat obediently near her right leg.

Nick's brows rose. Lately, Snowflake had been shadowing Holly whenever he was around her. Normally his dog was always walking at his right side, or with him. This change was unusual, but he wasn't disturbed by it. Snowflake had taken to Holly, just as he had. Maybe his dog knew more than he did? There was something new and provocative in her eyes earlier, as if she didn't want him to leave. He'd found out through Myra, weeks earlier, in a conversation that Holly had no man in her life presently, and hadn't for at least a year. She told him about the local accountant who was smug and arrogant with her, and that she'd quit seeing him. Maybe her comment about him having a kind face had something more behind it? Nick hadn't seen this accountant, James Westmore, in town yet. Did she keep herself busy so she wouldn't have time for any kind of relationship?

Watching from the table, he saw six children, ages seven to eleven, all crowd in and eagerly pet friendly Snowflake. His best friend loved children, but he always had, even over in Afghanistan. An idea slowly gelled in his mind. When Holly closed the door, coming to sit down and finish off her meal, he decided to ask her.

"My parents and I are having Thanksgiving at our home. Would you like to come over and be with us? I know we have to deliver turkey dinners from about four p.m. to the shut-ins, but after that?" he asked, holding her gaze.

"Did Sue invite me?" she asked a bit nervously.

"Uh . . . no. I'm inviting you, Holly." He saw surprise and then happiness gleam in her eyes.

"Oh, I'd love that. Thank you!"

He finished off his food, placing the plate aside. "I know you don't have family here, but I wasn't sure if you were going somewhere else for the holiday."

"No . . . I don't have anywhere to go. Usually, I spend time with the shut-ins, keeping them company, listening to their great stories and adventures about when they were younger."

Trying to tamp down his enthusiasm, he said, "I know my parents would love to have you with us."

"I would love to be there with all of you. Thank you."

He heard a slight quaver in her tone, saw a sheen of tears for a moment in her eyes and then, it was gone. How badly he wanted to wrap his arms around Holly. "I guess I can't even imagine what it would be like to lose both of my parents." Shaking his head, he offered, "But you know, you can consider my parents like your own."

Reaching out, Holly touched his forearm for a fleeting moment. "I know that, Nick. Your mom and dad are two of the most generous people in town."

"Mom closes up the diner for Thanksgiving because she wants to cook for us at home."

"And I'm glad she does that. Sue doesn't get much time off, either."

"Not if you own a small business," Nick agreed. "Well then, it's settled. We'll go over to my folks' home about six p.m. on Thanksgiving."

"Yes, that's wonderful. We'll have everything done around the charity and all my elders fed and happy, with pumpkin pie for dessert. Is there something I should bring for the dinner?"

"No, thanks. Just yourself. For once, let someone else do the cooking and you just enjoy your time with all of us."

CHAPTER 4

THE MID-NOVEMBER SKY was dark, flakes falling heavily as Nick drove the van back to the charity on slushy, wet Main Street. He was concerned about Holly, who had been distracted since he'd come in to help her mid-afternoon. It wasn't like her to be forgetful. She hadn't been her normal, upbeat self with the elders tonight, either. Snowflake, who now had fallen completely under her spell, remained close to her. Nick wished he had his dog's ability to read subtle human emotions. If only his dog could talk.

The sulfur lights highlighted the plowed snow pushed up along the two-lane highway between the center of town and the Delos charity. All the shops were closed by five p.m. during the winter months. In the summer, when tourists came, the shops remained opened until nine p.m. For the small business owners, tourists' money during the summer months tided them over through the slack months of winter. And Nick knew winter could stick around for a long time in the mountains of western Montana.

"Are you feeling okay?" he asked Holly, catching her shadowed gaze as the lights flashed through the windshield.

"I'm just . . . well . . . just thinking about something," she murmured.

Frowning, he took a left onto a side street where the charity was located. The street had yet to be plowed by the city's only snow plow. Slowing, he drove carefully. Luckily, Holly had hired a college student who worked by the hour to keep their large parking lot clear of snow. "Are you feeling okay? I mean, do you have a cold coming on or something?"

She shifted in the seat nervously. Then, she suggested, "Why don't you come over for a cup of hot chocolate after we get home, Nick? I'll tell you more about it then, okay?"

"Sure," he said, trying to curb his concern. Snowflake, who rode in the back seat, whined, which wasn't like him. This was something serious, he realized. Over the last few months, he'd grown closer to Holly and knew that she wasn't one to open up much about her private life. However, he thought he knew what was going on: it was the loss of her parents during the holiday season.

How would he feel if the holidays were coming up and he had no home to go to, and no parents to share his life with? He couldn't even imagine such a scenario. How could Holly deal with it? Maybe the season brought up more of her grief and loss than usual. Nick wanted to be there for her in whatever capacity she'd allow him.

Shooing Holly from the van after they parked, he told her to go to her apartment and watched as Snowflake trotted along at her side. He quickly carried the empty boxes to the kitchen on the first floor, and saw that Myra had come in earlier and cleaned up everything. The kitchen was prepped for tomorrow morning. If he hadn't been working with Delos now, from afar, he wouldn't have had any idea what it took to run a charity. It was only as good as the people who volunteered their time and hearts to it, he realized.

Wanting to finish with business, Nick hurried to put the rest of the items away and closed up the kitchen for the night. His heart and mind centered on Holly. She brought such lightness, such happiness to him—and to everyone else. The shut-ins doted on her as if she were their beloved granddaughter. How they looked forward to her arrival—and of course, Snowflake had become the doggie star of their team. Nick didn't mind being the person who carried in everything, got the dinner ready on a tray, and brought it over to the elderly while Holly talked with them. He knew someday he'd be old, too. He hoped he never ended up like this, although from what Holly told him, these elders were far better off than many others who didn't have a local charity to support them.

Still, it was a lonely existence, and Nick was too much of a team person to think about sitting twenty-four hours a day in an apartment without anyone else to talk to or share things with. That was why Snowflake was so intrinsic to their little three-person team. This thought made him smile a little. Even his dog was more relaxed, and his PTSD was not as bad as before. Neither was Nick's. He wasn't sure how much of it was because of Holly, or whether he was simply adjusting to civilian life. He also had the love and support of his parents. Even though they couldn't understand his nightmares, flashbacks, or his emotional ups and downs, they were there for him. That counted for a lot!

Holly, however, had no one to fall back on when she was down or needed support. More and more, Nick wanted to be that person and they were growing closer every day. But as he hurried up the stairs to his apartment to get cleaned up before going to see her, he realized he wanted to become so much more than that to Holly.

The wind was picking up, the snowflakes striking his face after he cleaned up, changed clothes, and walked down the inside passageway toward Holly's apartment door. He knocked and she answered, Snowflake wagging his stubby tail in greeting, his blue eyes shining with happiness upon seeing his master once more.

"Come in," she said, stepping aside.

Nick came in, wiped his feet on the heavy rug, and hung his coat on a nearby hook. "Smells good," he told her, following her into the kitchen. Holly was making her fabulous hot chocolate in a saucepan, stirring in the various ingredients. She didn't like boxed or packaged foods, preferring to make things from scratch. He saw their two cups sitting at the table. "Can I help?"

"No," she said, forcing a slight smile. "Go sit down."

"I see you got the marshmallows out. One for Snowflake?" He grinned, trying to ease her serious expression.

"One for him. Want to grab the whipped cream out of the fridge for us?"

"Sure." He noticed Holly had put on her gray, loose sweatpants, her feet in a pair of comfy slippers. More than anything, he liked to see her shoulder length hair down and curling around her face.

He had changed into a pair of tan chinos and a clean, black jersey. Often, food would get on his clothes here and there as he helped feed the shut-ins. Boxes weren't the ideal way to transport the warmed aluminum containers with their plastic covers. More than once, Nick had opened one and spilled some of the contents on himself in the process. Tonight was no exception, although he was getting better at handling their meals. Snowflake always hung around and if a speck of food dropped to the floor by accident, he was there immediately to gobble it up. Nothing went to waste in his dog's world and he grinned at the thought.

Within minutes, they were sitting at the table, their elbows almost touching. Snowflake positioned himself between them, looking up at them expectantly. "So," Nick said, catching her gaze, "what's going on, Holly?"

"I haven't told you everything about Noelle," she admitted, her voice soft and hesitant. Wrapping her slender hands around the cup, she said, "I don't like talking about this because it always upsets me."

Nodding, he said, "You always talk about her in the past tense." He saw her lips press together for a moment.

"Yes," she murmured, lifting her chin, holding his gaze. "After our parents died, Noelle told me she was being given an honorable medical discharge. I didn't understand what it meant."

"It meant whatever her diagnosis, it was interfering with her ability to work in the military," Nick provided. "You said she had PTSD?"

"Yeah," Holly muttered, rubbing her face. "Really bad."

"Were you shocked when she told you she was no longer in the military?"

Miserably, Holly nodded. "Was I ever . . . I mean, it's all Noelle knew. She was a Navy medic. She was always so confident, believed she could do anything, Nick, and now, here she was broken."

Grimly, he reached out, tucking her hand into his for a moment. Nick cherished these moments with Holly because the trust between them had grown and she would sometimes reach out and touch his hand or arm. Squeezing her hand, he forced himself to release it and said, "PTSD breaks even the strongest person, Holly."

"But you don't seem broken by it, Nick. You can still function."

He snorted and shook his head. "There are days when I really struggle, Holly." He gave her a warm look. "On those days, you give me the strength I need to deal with it."

Her brows flew upward. "Really?"

"Yeah. Why are you giving me that look?" he asked with a grin, seeing her cheeks pink up.

"Well," she sputtered, "because with Noelle, my presence didn't help her at all. I know we were both grieving over the loss of our mom and dad."

"She had a double load to carry at that time," he offered gently.

"I honestly didn't realize it then," she said, giving him a worried look. "I should have . . ."

"Don't go there, Holly."

"Maybe if I'd been more sensitive to her situation, to her feelings . . ."

Gripping her hand once more, Nick said, "Listen to me, Holly. There was nothing you could have done to help her. PTSD is internalized by many and they can hold it inside of them and not show it to the world around them. But you said she was drinking alcohol, too?"

She squeezed his hand in return. "Yes, she drank heavily for weeks after the funeral. I tried to talk to her, tried to get her interested in living, helping her to look for a civilian job, but nothing worked, Nick. Nothing." She looked away, biting down on her lower lip, struggling.

Seeing the tears of frustration in her eyes, he kept holding her hand, now feeling damp and clammy within his. He could see the sadness in her eyes, and wanted to protect her from all the suffering in this world. "I know her pain, Holly, and I'm sure you loved her fiercely, just like you do everyone else. But love alone couldn't tamp down whatever she was feeling. Probably, there was a lot of anxiety and she was getting no relief except to drink."

"You're right. On a good day I tell myself that, Nick." She clung to his hand. "Today is the day my sister committed suicide. She went out in the woods and shot herself in the head. I found her suicide note on my dresser later that day."

Nick's eyes widened. He stared at her. "God . . . no . . ."

Her lower lip trembled. "It was horrible. The sheriff found her after I called him about the note she'd left. It just seemed like a nightmare, and although it's been three years since her death, every year on this day it brings everything back to me."

"What else can I do to help?" he asked, his voice thick with emotion. He saw Holly give him a mournful look, tears threatening to spill. He curved his hand more firmly around hers. He lifted his arm, placing it around her broken shoulders and she gave him such a grateful look.

"Just you being with me today helped me, Nick. Usually I collapse, cry off and on all day, and hide from the world." She gave him a weak, partial smile, wiping the tears from her eyes. "With you and Snowflake around me I just have more strength than I normally do. It's helped me so much."

"Let us help you." He gently rubbed her tense shoulders, smoothing his palm lightly back and forth across them, trying to comfort Holly.

Her voice quavered, her gaze locked on his.

"You are both so special to me . . . to my heart. I look at before you two walked into my life and what it was like. I was so lonely. Oh, I know I'm always busy and I'm an extrovert, and I love people. But inside . . . I was so lonely." Searching his eyes, she whispered, "You make me laugh, Nick. You think the jokes are funny that I tell our elders, you seem to know when I really need your touch. You don't realize just how much you help me."

Stunned by her whispered admissions, he stared at her, unable to speak for a moment. His feelings were in knots, unraveling in his heart in every crazy direction. She stroked his other hand with her fingers and it sent tiny jolts up his hand and into his lower arm. "We're good for one another," he began, catching her fingers. That was what Holly needed right now: touch and comfort. She had been stripped of her daily armor by the memories of her lost sister and he was sure, of her parents, bearing down on her. "Holly? Let's go to your living room and sit down on the couch. I'm going to hold you. Right now you need a little TLC."

"I'd like that, Nick."

His heart leapt. Releasing her hand and re-moving his arm from around her shoulders, he stood. "Come on," he invited, moving to the back of her chair and pulling it out for her. Snowflake's tail wriggled and he danced around them as Nick placed his hand in the small of Holly's back, guiding her toward the living room.

HOLLY HAD NEVER felt so safe as right now with Nick. The ache in her heart eased as he sat down on the couch. Choosing a corner, he guided her next to him, his arm going about her shoulders once again. It felt good to nestle her brow against his neck, her head resting against his broad shoulder. Unlike with other men, she trusted Nick fully. In the last months, he'd proven many times over that he wouldn't try to breach her boundaries unless she wanted him to. He'd earned her trust more than any other man she'd ever known. Closing her eyes, folded up against him, she placed her hand on his chest, his heart beneath her palm. "Thank you," she murmured, nuzzling his jaw. "I really needed this."

"Just rest, Holly. You need to stop pushing so hard all the time."

She laughed a little at Nick's low, concerned growl in his tone. "I warned you from the beginning I was a clone of the Energizer Bunny." She sighed as he squeezed her shoulders gently. Then, he slipped his hand over hers, now resting on his chest. There was such wonderful intimacy springing to life between them. She heard the rumble of a chuckle in his broad chest.

"Yes, you did warn me." Nick turned, his lips against her unruly red hair. "But on days like this you need to slow down and just take care of yourself first."

"I fall apart sometimes," she agreed.

"You didn't today, but I knew you were bothered about something."

"Snowflake sensed it, too." She pulled her head back to meet Nick's dark-green eyes. They held such tenderness in them right now, and all for her. "You two take really good care of me," she murmured gratefully, her gaze trailing to his strong, sculpted mouth.

There was nothing soft about Nick. There never had been, but he wasn't a bully and he wasn't loud or arrogant like so many men she had known. Instead, it was his confidence, his quiet strength that permeated every pore of his being. Holly knew why Snowflake adored him. Right now, Nick was holding her, asking nothing more of her than to offer her a safe, emotional harbor for just a bit. Her heart pounded, telling her how much more she wanted of him. She wanted to taste his lips against hers, feel his mouth brush against hers. Oh, she knew he would be a wonderful lover. Her lower body filled with need. Being around Nick nearly every day made her fully aware of her femininity and how unfulfilled she felt right now. But now wasn't the time to address this, and he seemed to sense that, too.

She felt him caress the back of her hand on his chest, as if soothing a child who was out of sorts and needed calming.

"You don't let anyone take care of you most of the time," Nick told her thickly. "I guess me and Snowflake are badass military protectors who want to do just that for you." One corner of his mouth curved as he admitted, "So this is really special for me, too, Holly. I like it."

She stared wonderingly up at him, lost in the depth of his jade eyes. Holly saw that Nick wanted to kiss her. It was right there, being silently offered to her. She could feel the moisture of his breath, he was that close to her. His arm tightened just a smidgen around her shoulders, as if to silently claim her as his own.

Did Holly want that more than anything? Yes! Her mind had dissolved in that heated moment strung sweetly and building swiftly between them. Instinctively, she leaned upward, telling him in an ancient language that needed no words that she wanted to kiss him, too. Her lashes swept downward as he dipped his head, his mouth softly engaging hers with invitation. Answering, opening to him, eager to merge with Nick, she felt his hand leave hers and rest upon her left shoulder, angling her more surely against him. Her breasts brushed his chest as a low moan echoed in her throat. She felt his mouth exploring, cajoling, asking her to join him in their dance of exploration and deepening intimacy with one another.

The moment he threaded his fingers through her hair just above her ear, thousands of tiny sparks ignited, sweeping through her. His tenderness extended to more than just the gentle exploration of her mouth. He was being gentle and careful right now, and never had Holly been held as if she were a sacred, adored woman. The sensation flowed through her, easing her grief for her sister, allowing her to literally sink into Nick's arms and fully trust him with herself in every way. In the back of her dissolving mind, she knew he would go no further than their kiss, or the caress of her silky hair. Something told her that he'd waited a long time to do just this. But hadn't she, too? Yes. Absolutely, yes.

As his mouth lifted from hers, Holly inhaled his male scent, now dizzy in her need for him. Barely lifting her lashes, she drowned in the heat she saw in his darkening eyes. There was no question that Nick, when necessary, could become a warrior at a moment's notice. She could feel him reining himself in for her sake, not wanting to use his superior strength against her. Rather, he was sensing her reactions, every last one of them.

What man had ever done that for her before? None. It was so easy to lose herself in his hungry, intense gaze. But she loved to experience how his fingers threaded through her hair, grazed her cheek, and then feel his thumb trace her wet, lower lip. He was literally memorizing her. She could feel it, and accepted his mapping her, from his heart to hers.

This was about so much more than just sex and hormones right now. Nick was a man who played for keeps. He didn't want just one night with her. He wanted her for a lifetime and he was serious about her and their budding relationship.

"That was," she said, her voice wispy, "wonderful." She instantly saw relief and then pride come to his eyes. Lifting her hand, she touched his roughened jaw. "I wanted you to kiss me so much, Nick."

"I thought so," he admitted gruffly, "but I wasn't sure. I'm glad you took the lead," and he caressed the top of her head.

"Because you weren't sure about me? Us?"

"I always thought my liking you was probably one-sided, Holly. I was never sure that you felt the same way toward me as I did you." One corner of Nick's mouth hooked upward. "When it comes to reading signals in a woman, I don't always read them right."

"You sure did this time," she said, fingertips touching her lower lip.

"That's just another thing to like about you," he offered. "You're honest and I love that about you." His hand stilled over her hair. "Holly, ever since I met you, I always thought you were some magical creature come to save my worthless hide. You lifted me up out of the quagmire I was trapped in. You gave me hope again, and I looked forward to being with you every day that I could. I always felt better when you were around me. Life just looked better. I don't have the words, but you've affected me in the best of ways."

Her hand stilled against his jaw. "You do the same for me, Nick. From the very beginning when we met, that's how I felt about you."

Snowflake, who sat watching them, just outside where their feet rested, whined, his stub and rear wriggling madly with enthusiasm.

Holly smiled and eased upward as Nick's arm moved to lightly curve around her waist. She reached out, petting Snowflake's head. "He must have known, Nick. About us."

"Dogs always read a person's heart and emotions," he admitted, giving her a tender look.

She straightened, feeling euphoric, cared for, and desired. "Where do we go from here?"

"Where do you want it to go, Holly? I'm open to whatever is comfortable for you. I'm not the kind of guy who has a string of women—it's not who I am, but I think you already knew that."

"I know your family well, Nick. Your dad is faithful to your mom, Sue. He adores her. I see him do small, meaningful things for her every time we're together. I'm sure you would be the same way because that's how he raised you."

"My dad made a huge impact in my life," Nick agreed. "He was the one who taught me to respect a woman, and not play games with her. I got several talks when I turned thirteen. But I'd already seen how he treated my mother. He's always been my role model."

"When I was kissing you, I was thinking how unlike you were compared to most other guys." She saw him cock his head, a question in his gaze. "You didn't take from me, Nick. You offered something to me and then waited to see if I wanted it or not. Most guys will grab a kiss whether I want him to or not."

"Oh," he said, "Well, that was talk 101 with my dad. He made it clear that a woman has her own mind and needs. And that whatever she wanted with me, she'd let me know. Then, I could react to it." He shrugged. "It's something I practiced when I was in a relationship during the military. I won't take from you, Holly, without giving you back the same, or more, from myself."

"I could tell with just that kiss, Nick. I liked it a lot. I felt like I was a true partner in what we have."

"You always will be."

She heard the depth of his promise to her, saw it in his eyes, that commitment, that adoration of her as a woman of equal worth. "You asked me where I wanted to go with us?"

"Yes."

"Can we just let this unfold naturally between us over time? We're both so busy that I feel it would be best that way. What do you want to do?"

He smiled a little, watching the light glance off her tousled red hair. "Sounds good to me. A day at a time."

SNOW WAS COMING down hard in town as Nick drove the van toward the shut-in area at four p.m. The smell of spaghetti and buttered, garlic toast filled the vehicle. Myra had made sweet potato cupcakes for dessert, and he stole one before they left the charity facility. It was nearly Thanksgiving and he was looking forward to taking Holly to his folks place for the afternoon and evening. The wipers were rhythmically swinging back and forth, throwing off the heavy, wet flakes. The roads were salted, but still Nick was wary of invisible black ice. In the late afternoon the heat of the day was gone and things got slick real fast.

"Oh dear," Holly called, sitting up, pointing out her passenger-side window. "Look, Nick!"

Snowflake, who stood between them, heard the pitch of her voice change, and whined.

Nick slowed and pulled over to the curb, then looked to where she was pointing. There was a yellow Labrador moving awkwardly through the belly deep snow between two brick buildings. Her ribs were prominent even though she had a short, thick winter coat on. "She's starving," he muttered, scowling. "It looks like a female Lab. She's too dainty looking to be a male."

"She's terribly thin," Holly said, worried. "I wonder if someone dumped her—they do that all the time around here. I hate it."

"No collar on her, either," Nick agreed. The Lab was about a hundred-feet down the alley between the two buildings, slugging it out with the snow. Nick heard Holly make a little sound of urgency. She had such a big heart, and she hated to see animals or humans suffer.

Nick knew she wanted to get out and try to call the dog over to her. From the looks of the animal, her light-brown eyes wild looking, tongue lolling out of her mouth, her fur matted, he intuitively knew this was a dog that had been left behind a long time ago to fend for herself.

"She's feral," he warned Holly. She turned, her huge, blue eyes filled with tears. "She won't let us near her. I'm sorry." And he was. It wouldn't be the first dog dumped here that Nick had found, or that Holly had come upon around the building of one of her shut-ins. They had a no-kill shelter here, and this Lab would have had a warm place to stay, food, and care if they could befriend her.

"Can't we do something for her, Nick?"

He put the van in park. "Yeah," he said, getting up and moving between the seats. "Didn't Myra pack some extra meatballs for the elders? She was thinking along the line of making them sandwiches tomorrow at noon." He leaned over the different boxes, opening each one of them and peering inside.

"Yes, she did." Holly turned, watching him. "What are you going to do?"

"I'll put the meatballs out and hope she'll smell them in the alley and come back and eat them. We can't give her too much, Holly. As starved as she is, she'll gobble it all down and then vomit it all right back up."

Making a sad sound, she twisted around. "Wait! She's standing at the end of the alley, looking at us!"

"She probably smells the food in the van," Nick said, grabbing the bag of meatballs. Straightening a little, he opened the side door on the van. "I'll be right back."

As Nick walked slowly toward the alley, he thought how much the female looked like Dude. A feminine version of him, for sure. She watched him warily, taking a step or two back, but her eyes stayed on the bag in his hand.

Nick spoke softly to her, hoping his voice would calm her, not scare her. He knelt down at the entrance fifty-feet between them. Nick opened the bag and dumped the meat into the snow. Looking up, he saw her licking her chops. Yeah, she smelled the meat. That was good.

"Come on, Lady," he called softly to her, slowly rising and backing away. "Come and get your dinner. We're not going to hurt you. Come on, girl."

Turning slowly so as not to startle her, he walked back to the van. By the time he got to it and turned, the Labrador had run up to where the food had been, gulped it, and then ran back down the alley and disappeared. The dog was potentially beautiful once she got cleaned up and fattened up a bit. Nick could tell she wanted to come to him, but fear kept her from doing that.

Climbing into the van, he dropped the Ziploc into one of the nearby boxes behind his seat.

"As soon as you turned away from her," Holly said, "the dog came running up. I don't think she even chewed the meatballs, Nick. She just gulped them in a huge bite, whirled around, and raced down the alley."

"Which way did she go?" Nick asked.

"To the left. It seemed like she knew where she was going."

Snowflake whined, coming between the seats, smelling Nick's hip and thigh. Smelling the other dog's scent on him.

"He was whining all the time," Holly told him, petting the shepherd. "It was like he knew what was going on."

"He probably did," Nick agreed. "Okay, now we need to get to our shut-ins," he said, putting the van in gear. As he drove slowly down the highway of the town, early Christmas decorations crisscrossing Main Street, his mind and heart were centered on Lady. Yeah, he'd named her, which wasn't a good sign. But she was a beautiful yellow Lab, with a broad, fine looking head and large, intelligent golden-brown eyes. Just like Dude. She was a spitting image of him in so many ways, even the shape and length of her muzzle. "Have you seen her around here before?" he asked Holly.

Shaking her head, she said, "No, this is the first time."

"Someone probably dumped her awhile back, she's so thin and ratty looking. She's come in close to the town to find food, probably digging in garbage cans, overturning them, trying to find something so she won't starve to death. She knows that wolves, coyotes, or foxes are nearby, which is why she's hiding in town."

"Can't we do something? I could call Elaine over at the no-kill shelter. Maybe they could catch her?"

"She's wild, Holly. She's not trusting of any

humans, at all. The dog wouldn't come if you called her."

Moaning, she whispered, "But it's near zero degrees tonight, Nick. Couldn't we find her? Could you track her?"

"I could, yes, with Snowflake. But if she heard us coming she'd take off. Chances are she's got a nest under a building or a sidewalk where she's out of the snow and most of the cold."

"Well, can't we do something?" insisted Holly. She was not taking no for an answer.

"You pass by that alley three times a day. You and I could leave her a bowl of dried food, and a small pan of warm water. Right now, she's starved and probably needing hydration. Her fur is tight on her body and that means she's not drinking enough water. She'll eat snow, but it'll freeze her tongue and mouth and she'll stop eating it. She's not getting enough water down her."

"We could do that!" Holly said, suddenly hopeful. "Can you show me how much I should give her if you're not with me?"

"Yeah. If we could start feeding her three times a day in the alley, she would come back into it and check it at those times of day. We could talk to the businesses in both buildings and let them know what we're doing."

"Oh, that's the Henderson's and the Johnson's. They both have dogs. They wouldn't mind if we tried to befriend her and got her to a shelter."

"What I want to do is get Lady . . . I mean . . . the yellow Lab, to expect her food daily. That way, at some point, we can stand a short distance away from her after we bring the food and she could start to learn to trust us. We can talk to her in soft voices. Then, she might eventually come to us so we can put her some-place warm and safe."

"Lady. Is that what you named her? I love the name. It suits her perfectly. She's so delicate and beautiful."

Nick grinned shyly. "She's a very pretty Lab, really well-built, and feminine looking."

Reaching over, Holly squeezed his upper arm, beaming at him. "I just love the name, Lady. It really does suit her perfectly! I wonder if she smiles like Dude?"

CHAPTER 5

November 26

H OLLY WANTED TO look especially pretty tonight and critically examined herself in the mirror. Her choice of outfit for Thanksgiving dinner was a red, velvet dress. She smoothed her hand down the simple line of the empire-waistline dress that fell to the middle of her knees. The long sleeves were cuffed, a pearl button on each one. Most of all, she loved the white, crocheted collar. This was a vintage dress from the 1960s that she'd bought from Candy's Antique Shop a year ago. It was a perfect match to her carrot-colored hair.

The white, delicate crocheted collar, however, was special and she continued to touch it briefly with her fingertips. Tonight, she'd put her hair up on her head with an antique, tortoiseshell clip given to her by her grandmother when she was a child. Her mother had given her a set of small, white pearl earrings for her twelfth birthday, telling her that every young woman should own at least one pair.

The knock on her door made her turn and she quickly picked up her crocheted white purse that matched the collar, hurrying to the door. Dinner would be served at seven p.m. at the Conway residence. She was a little nervous, wanting to look pretty for Nick, and took a deep breath as she opened the door.

Holly gasped. Nick was dressed in a dark-brown corduroy sports coat, a cream colored shirt, and tan slacks. His hair was sleek and she knew he'd taken a shower earlier. All that scruff was gone, too. She grinned. "Wow, Conway, you clean up well. Come in!" She saw his cheeks grow ruddy over her compliment.

"You look stunning in that red, velvet dress," he said, giving her a pleasant up-and-down look of appreciation. "You know, this is the first time I've seen you in a dress, Holly."

It was her turn to feel heat fly into her cheeks as she closed the door. "I clean up pretty well, like you, when there's a reason to do it." She twirled around in the dress. "I feel like a fairytale princess, to tell you the truth." Holly could see from his penetrating look that he was tempted to kiss her, and a thrill of anticipation shot through her. Nick made her feel beautiful, even though she knew she wasn't—not with all her freckles and this untamed, curly red hair of hers.

"I need to take you out more often, then. That collar is beautiful."

"Oh," she said, touching it gently, "my grandma, Esmeralda, created it. Back in her day this kind of collar was in vogue. I'm glad she passed it on to me because I just love it. It's so frilly and feminine."

"Sure gives a new meaning to that dress you're wearing," he agreed amiably. "I like that you have special things from your family passed on to you. That's important."

"These pearl earrings were given to me by my mother," she said, looking at the watch on her right wrist. "I'm ready to go. Could you help me on with my good, gray wool coat?"

He smiled. "Sure."

"I'll be right back. Oh, and this purse? My grandma crocheted that, too. Isn't it pretty?" She placed it in his hands, hurrying down the hall to her bedroom to retrieve her coat from the closet.

Nick smiled, holding the small, delicate-looking purse with a long strap. He was holding a piece of Holly's family history, which warmed his heart. When she returned with the gray coat over her arm, he said, "You outshine this purse, believe me. Those pearl earrings look like antiques. Are they?" He eased the coat from her and she turned around.

"Yes, my mom bought them at an antique store in Billings, Montana and gave them to me on my twelfth birthday," she said, easing her hands into the coat sleeves. Turning after Nick brought the coat up around her, she picked up her dark-green knit scarf, her black gloves, and took the purse from his hands.

"You remind me of a woman from the late 1800s, except that your dress is so short."

She tittered as he opened the door. "I do love what my family gave me. It always makes me feel loved, like they're here with me in spirit."

Nick locked her apartment door and handed her the keys. "I'm sure they are. I hope you have an appetite tonight, Ms. McGuire."

"Oh, I'm starving!" She wanted to add: for you, but didn't have the courage to say it to Nick. At least, not yet. She slipped her hand through his arm and he drew her close as they walked toward the stairwell. "Aren't we taking Snowflake tonight?"

"No, he's on his doggy cushion in the kitchen. He'll be fine until we get home."

Holly nodded. When Nick took her to the movie, bowling, or to the small shopping mall for a meal, he left his dog at home. The night sky was clear now, stars glimmering, a nearly full moon upon them. Earlier, the snow had coated everything in town white once more. To Holly, this town reminded her of a Christmas postcard from the late 1800s. It was odd that Nick would choose that time to describe her, but it made her feel good. In so many ways, they were in tune with one another.

As he slowed at the stairs, she said, "Lady is getting used to us a little, I think. Tonight, when you brought her some leftover turkey for her dinner, she was waiting for you at the end of the alley."

"Yeah, and she thumped her tail in the snow. I liked seeing that."

"What does it mean, do you think?"

"That she's glad to see me. Does she wag her tail for you, yet?"

"Yes, sometimes. But it can get a bit busy at noon with people walking by, and she usually leaves because strangers passing by the entrance area make her nervous."

As they came off the stairs and on the clean sidewalk sprinkled with salt, Nick said, "I'm going to try something new tomorrow. I'm going to bring Snowflake out with me on the leash. I want Lady to see that my dog likes me and isn't afraid of me. It might help her relax and trust me a little more."

"That sounds like a great idea!" Holly agreed, suddenly excited. Tonight, Nick was driving them to dinner. He opened the door for her and she slid in, tucking the dress and coat around herself.

Nick got in and she breathed in his male

scent. It made her want to touch him, kiss him, and . . . Holly wasn't about to admit that since their kiss two weeks earlier, she'd wanted to do it again. Okay, so they hadn't, but other nice things had happened between them since. She had sexual dreams of loving Nick and she often woke up, her heart beating crazily, her lower body aching for his touch.

He touched her more often now, in a friendly, warm way. Nothing sexually suggestive, but as if the kiss had broken down a barrier that had lain between them earlier. He laughed more with her. They joked around frequently with one another. Maybe her red hair was her downfall. She was in a hurry to create more intimacy and friendship between them.

Nick was unveiling himself to her a little more each day and she craved his trust in her because she trusted him. Sometimes, Holly wished she wasn't so darned impatient and always in a hurry. Nick was the opposite: slow, steady, and sure. That was probably why he'd been a military dog handler. She'd never make that grade, either.

"You've fed Lady at least half the time," Nick said, slowly driving the car out of the snow covered parking lot. "She seems less afraid of you. Have you noticed that?"

"She doesn't tense up as much. And she's quicker to come to me than you," she agreed.

"I think a man badly abused her. I think Lady considers you safer than me because you're a female."

Shrugging, Holly said, "Well, I love her and maybe that's what she feels. But I know you love her, too, from a distance," she said, catching his shadowed glance as he guided the vehicle onto Main Street.

"I've watched her closely," he murmured, "and I'm just wondering if you should be with me when I feed her next time. If she sees us together, she might see us as a pack, alpha male and female, so to speak. And by adding Snowflake to the mix, providing she gets along with him, she might feel more willing to trust us more. Every dog wants to belong to a pack."

"Those ancient wolf genes, right?" Holly teased, reaching out, moving her gloved hand down his forearm. Tonight, Nick looked utterly delicious. She had wanted him in her bed, and if her dreams got any hotter, she'd burn up the sheets! Compressing her lips, she moved her hand on his hard thigh, feeling his muscles leap in response to her light touch. It was time to become more obvious because Nick seemed not to be reading her subtle messages. Maybe she was being too subtle for him.

"Yes, wolf genes," Nick agreed. He kept his hands on the steering wheel, making a left onto the street where his parents' home was located.

The flakes were becoming almost horizontal, the blasts of wind accompanying the deep cold front sweeping across the area, shaking the car.

"I like being the alpha female in our relationship," she said, watching his smile grow.

"Snowflake has already accepted you as part of his pack." He grinned, "To him, you're just another sheep to herd around."

"You're a sheep, too, but the ram of the herd," she teased.

Nick slowed down to a driveway that had been recently cleared but was quickly adding snow to it once again. "That's true."

"I like the idea of being in a pack with you, Nick," she said. Her obvious statement couldn't be missed and she watched him out of the corner of her eye as he turned into his parents' single-story ranch home. Chet had decorated it weeks earlier with Christmas lights strung along the roof gutters. She loved Christmas and all that it meant and held for her and her lost family.

Parking the car, Nick took off his seat belt and leaned over, sliding his arm around her shoulders, giving her a light kiss on the lips. "Then," he growled, holding her gaze, "we need to make this night special." Releasing her, he gave her a dark look that held a wonderful promise.

NICK DIDN'T LIKE the ferocity of the blizzard as they left his parents' home after a wonderful evening. He bundled Holly up, shielding her with his body as he led her to the car. They had eaten turkey with all the fixings, laughed a lot, joked, and he felt she had genuinely become a part of their family. His heart swelled with need of Holly in every way. Just looking at her from across the table, he found her unbelievably beautiful. Now, snowflakes melted in her hair even though his mother had given Holly a large scarf to protect her head on their run to the car.

"Wow, this is a real storm!" Holly said, once inside.

Nick backed out of the driveway, snow crunching beneath the tires. "I remember them like this. That cold front from Alaska sweeps down across the northwest and it hits our mountains and it dumps across it, right on top of us."

Taking off the scarf, she shook her head, snowflakes falling here and there around her, quickly melting. "I just worry about Lady on nights like this, Nick."

"I know," he mused, driving slowly, the headlights glaring on the snow across the two-lane street. "We don't know where she stays, but I'm sure she's smart enough to find something to curl up into that is out of the wind. There's a lot of garage stuff behind Mr. Henderson's three-story brick building. Lots of hidey holes."

"I know," she said, sliding her hand up and down his thigh, "but I still worry."

He clasped her hand, lifting it, and placing a kiss on the back of it. "You have such a large heart, Holly. Lady will be okay. She knows how to hunker down."

"I so wish she'd come home with us. I'd love to add her to our little family."

Nick squeezed her hand and released it, ready to make the turn onto Main Street. "She's feral, Holly. But the good news is, she's gained weight and her ribs aren't so prominent. We're helping her, so feel good about what we can do for her, okay?"

"I do," she whispered. Lifting her hand, she moved it across the shoulders of his damp jacket. She knew she was falling in love with this man who cared so deeply for everyone. Moving her fingers across his broad shoulder, she said, "I don't want to sleep alone tonight, Nick," and her hand stilled on his jacket as she watched his reaction.

He cut her a glance. "You're sure, Holly?"

"Very sure. You?"

His mouth crooked and he gave her a tender look. "I've been wanting to have you in my bed, in my arms, since I met you."

Holly nodded, allowing his low, thick tone to flow through her, igniting that place deep within her body where she always found herself aching for his touch. "Funny," she mused, "when I saw you the first time I felt like I knew you. It was as if you were stepping back into my life and we were going to continue our relationship with one another. I guess it was a crazy thought, but that's how I felt about you."

He turned into the charity parking lot, now covered with nearly a foot of fresh snow. The wind had lessened for a while, the snow no longer fell in horizontal sheets, but it was still falling quickly and heavily. Parking the car, he said, "Your place or mine?"

"Yours, I guess. You have Snowflake to think about."

"Oh," Nick said wryly, unbuckling his seat belt, "he sleeps out on his fluffy, cozy doggy cushion in the corner of the kitchen. The bedroom door will be closed and it will be just you and me."

She smiled. "Do you think it will upset Snowflake to have me over there with you?"

"Nah," Nick said, "he loves you as much as he loves me. He'll be glad to see you with me."

Smiling, she got rid of the seat belt. "Let's go up. You have to take him out to do his business, don't you?"

"Yep."

"I'm going to get out of these clothes and into something comfortable and then I'll come over."

He gave her a burning look. "You have no idea how much that dress has turned me on, sweetheart."

Feeling her cheeks heat up, she watched him leave the car. It was the first time he'd used an endearment, and it meant the world to Holly. Waiting, Nick came around and opened the door for her, his gloved hand extended toward her. She took it, loving his courtly manner. Every nerve in her body was on fire and expectant. At last! She was going to be with Nick all night! It seemed like a miracle, a wonderful one to Holly as she stepped out of the car and into another chapter of their lives together.

IT WAS AS if she were in one of her torrid dreams with Nick, only this one was real. Holly felt like a beautiful princess as he began to undress her. Because he liked her velvet, red dress, she had kept it on. She'd removed her shoes and nylons and was now barefoot, standing in his arms, looking up at him. He, too, had removed his shoes, and was now in his sock feet, and that made her smile. He'd changed into a long-sleeved dark-blue tee and jeans. The way he looked at her, with his all-consuming gaze, made her feel deliciously desired. She moved her hands slowly up and down his upper arms.

"Are you nervous?" she asked, watching his mouth crook.

"More than a little. It's been a long time since I made love with a woman, Holly. And I know it's been some time for you, too."

"I feel better that we can be nervous together. Why did we wait so long?" she wondered, as she absorbed the strength of his arms beneath that soft fabric. Her heart thudded as he gave her a heated look.

"We need to take our time. That will help quiet our worries and nerves," he murmured, moving his hands upward to unclip her red hair from behind her head. Her thick, silky strands tumbled around her shoulders.

Holly saw the pleasure gleam in Nick's eyes as he watched her hair fall free. He laid the antique clip on a nearby dresser. Returning to her, he smoothed his hands across her shoulders, easing her hair to her back, watching her expression. Her skin rippled with shivery delight as he opened the pearl button behind her nape, loosening the dress and collar. Next came the zipper, which he nudged down slowly, his fingers trailing along her spine, inciting more fire within her lower body.

Her nerves faded beneath his exploring hands as he brushed them beneath the nubby fabric and his callouses grazed her awakening flesh. The shoulders of the dress fell away and she stepped back, allowing him to draw the sleeves off her arms and hands. Nick caught the dress, not allowing it to fall onto the floor. Instead, he gripped her left elbow and helped her step out of it.

"This is too pretty to lay on the floor," he told her, releasing her and draping the fabric across the top of a chair. Turning, he held her gaze. "Do you know how gorgeous you are?"

Holly shook her head, feeling her whole being react to that low growl of his, his gaze consuming her once more from head to toe. "No, but I'm glad you like what you see."

"I do, very much," and he lifted the tee off and pulled it over his head. He placed it on the seat of the chair. Next came his jeans.

She had never seen his powerful legs, but her eyes were drawn to his boxer shorts, to the erection pressed against the material. Nick was just as beautiful in her eyes as she was to him. He was strong, well built, all muscle with not an ounce of fat on him. Making quick work of his dark blue socks, he straightened and walked over, enclosing her loosely within his arms.

"There, now we're even." He moved his hands to behind her bra, opening it, pulling the straps down her shoulders to her arms.

Her breath caught as her filmy, white silk bra fell away, revealing her breasts to him. Nick's eyes grew dark and she could tell he more than liked what he saw. Trailing her fingers down through the dusting of dark hair across his well sprung chest, he tensed.

"You have no idea how good you feel to me," he groaned.

She smiled a little, stepping away, easing her silky panties off her legs. "Oh," she murmured, giving him a wry glance at his erection, "I think I do." Her heart was in the mix as she gripped his hand, leading him to the bed. "I want to fulfill my dreams with you, Nick," she whispered. "It's time."

If her dreams were torrid, the real life movement of his roughened hands across her flesh made her sizzle and ache. Because he was concerned with her comfort, he was lying on his back, lifting her up and over him. As her thighs bracketed his narrow hips, she settled on the warm, hard steel of his erection, her wetness gliding against him, making her moan in appreciation. She closed her eyes, pleasure zinging through her.

His hands cupped her small breasts and she leaned into his roughened palms. Feeling him pressing against her entrance, Holly was able to ease slowly down upon Nick, giving her body the time it needed to stretch and adjust. Even that movement heightened her building need of him. And when he framed her face, entrapping her, and drawing her down to his awaiting mouth, it was like melting wax meeting a red hot flame.

Nick lifted his hips as he drank her deeply into him, his mouth coaxing, strong and hungry, she lost all coherent thoughts, her hands pressed to his shoulders, a moan deep in her throat. His kiss was strong, cajoling, and as he slid into her, she became mindless, allowing her heart to lead her, instead. Even her dreams couldn't rival his adoration of her and when Nick coaxed her first orgasm out of her, she cried out, raw pleasure tearing through her, rippling, making her soar into a heady atmosphere where only the glimmering stars existed.

His tenderness toward her continued as he later eased her onto her back, bringing him to climax. She had a second orgasm that nearly brought her to tears. Holly wasn't sure where she was as that second orgasm exploded through her lower body. She felt Nick's warm, strong arms cosseting her, their bodies fused in heat and molten pleasure, sending her somewhere beautiful where she'd never been before. Feeling almost faint from the intensity of the releases, his male scent surrounding her, his moist breath across her brow and mussed hair, fed her satiated body. Afterward, he'd eased out of her and pulled her into his arms.

How long she slept afterward, Holly had no idea. Nick's soft breath against her nape, his arm around her waist, holding her close, brought simmering joy to her. He had spooned his body around hers, the thick, goose-down cover over them, warm. It was his quiet strength as he held her, protecting her, that was exclusive to their coupling, and Holly didn't want this to end. She had loved Nick last night with everything she had, showing him without words, but with her body, just how much he meant to her.

Had she been hearing things as she drifted off to sleep? She swore she heard Nick whisper against her hair that he loved her—or had she made it up? Was it what she wanted to hear, not what he'd said?

Nick was perfect for her. Holly knew he had up and down days with his PTSD, his anxiety came and went, and she knew it would probably never go away. But he worked with her, communicated with her, telling her when he was feeling rough. Most men didn't tell women that sort of thing, but he had, and Holly knew it meant that he trusted her, and that he knew she would be sensitive to when he was in a vulnerable state.

As she lay there in his embrace, his one arm beneath her neck, her back pressed to his chest and lower body, she luxuriated in their quiet moment. Did Nick love her? Did he really say those words? Or had she imagined hearing those words from him? If Nick knew of her dreams for them, he would probably just shake his head and give her that mirthful look of his. His eyes danced with amusement over her girlish spontaneity, but now, Holly realized that he enjoyed those moments. Was he regaining that childlike ability he'd lost in combat? She thought so, but wasn't sure. At least, not yet.

Sighing softly, she felt Nick's arm tighten marginally.

"I can hear you thinking, Holly," he mumbled into her hair.

Hearing the smile in his voice, her lips lifted. "How could you know that?"

Stretching, Nick released her and moved her such that she was on her back, looking up at him, his long body against hers. "I could feel you thinking."

"Hmmm," she said, grazing the stubble across his cheek, "are you more dog than man? Dogs can feel all our emotions and know exactly what we're feeling."

He leaned down, pressing a kiss to her brow. "I don't know. I've always seemed to have this invisible connection with you, Holly. From the day I met you, I wanted you to be mine." His green eyes darkened as he held her luminous ones. "And you are."

"I want more of you, more sharing, Nick. Don't you?" It took all her courage to ask, but Holly knew if she didn't, she'd waffle, worry, and drive herself crazy. She wasn't sure what she'd do if Nick said no. He'd loved her so well last night, as if she were this priceless, one-of-a-kind being, and she felt her heart explode with what she knew to be love for him. Watching his face, those sculpted lips of his curve, that deviltry enter his eyes, she relaxed, knowing the answer was yes.

"I've wanted exactly what we're sharing right now with you from the get-go, Holly. I won't lie to you. I saw you and it was lust." Nick picked up a strand of her crimson hair, nudging it away from her cheek. "You were this red-haired vixen-fairy. At least, that's how I saw you the first time we met." He smoothed the curl up and over her delicate ear. "The more I discovered about you, the more my heart became involved, as well."

"I've become more than just a bedmate?"

"That and so much more," he admitted thickly, holding her shimmering gaze. "When I wake up in the morning I know you're close by. I know I'll probably get to spend all or part of a day with you because of my classes." He caressed her warm, flushed cheek. "You grew into my heart, Holly. You possess my heart."

Her lips parted, her heart thundering suddenly as she stared disbelievingly into his intense gaze. "Then," she whispered, "I wasn't wrong."

"Wrong about what?"

"I thought I heard you whisper that you loved me just before I dropped off to sleep in your arms, after we made love." She saw his mouth curve, a gleam in his green eyes.

"I did. And I do love you, Holly McGuire."

CHAPTER 6

December 12

"THERE SHE IS!" Holly said excitedly. Every day, they made three stops between the two red-brick business buildings to see if Lady was at the other end of it, waiting for them to deliver her food. Today, two weeks after they had made love for the first time, Nick was now on Christmas break from college. He was driving her to her shut-ins three times daily and she loved having his company. Snowflake stood between the two seats of the van, whining because he knew what they were going to do.

Nick slowed and pulled over to the curb. The snow lay in the alley and he could see Lady waiting for them at the other end. "Good," he said, putting the van in park. "Are you ready to try our next step in trying to get her to come to us?"

"You bet," Holly said eagerly.

"Lady is less skittish around you," Nick said. "I'm going to put Snowflake on his long leash and we'll go out together. I'll want you to go put the food down for her and let's see what she does."

"Do you think seeing Snowflake will scare her off?"

"I don't know. But you go put the food where you always do and then back off and stay with us. We'll see how she responds."

Trying to contain her excitement, Holly climbed out. Nick put the leash on Snowflake, now practically leaping up and down in the back of the van. They had just finished their lunch route for their shut-ins and were on their way back to the charity. The van's doors slid open on both sides and Nick led Snowflake out one side while Holly got the bowl of dried food and sprinkled some leftover turkey on top of it for Lady.

It was cold, in the twenties, the wind blowing through the valley where Hamilton sat. As she pulled the plastic dog bowl into her gloved hands, she was glad to have her thick, knitted cap on her hair and a muffler around her neck. It hadn't snowed since last week, much of it melting, making it easy to walk between the two buildings.

Nick kept Snowflake on a short leash at his side, their boots crunching on the snow as they moved into the alley. He was glad to know that the five-thousand people who lived in this small mountain town knew they were trying to coax Lady into becoming tame enough so that they could get her into the no-kill shelter. He saw her at the other end, watching them. Her ears perked up at seeing Snowflake at his side.

"She's spotted Snowflake," he told Holly, who walked a few-feet away from them.

"Yes, and she looks really alert about it." She gave Nick a warm look. "I think she's lonely. Maybe not for humans, but for another dog who could be her companion?"

"I don't know." He halted and said, "Go to your regular spot where you feed her and come back. Let's see what she does."

Following his directions, Holly walked forward, speaking softly to Lady, who seemed to know her name. She stood waiting, her gaze fixed on the bowl in Holly's hands. Crouching down, Holly put the bowl up against one brick building. She had a second bowl and a thermos of warm water for the dog, as well. It took her about five minutes to get the water into the other bowl. Glancing down the alleyway, she saw Lady had come forward. Thrilled, she smiled.

"Hi, sweetie," she called. "Come and get your food and water. Some nice turkey is waiting for you."

Lady was within six-feet of her. Holly smiled

at the Lab looking her over. The dog had gained weight from their feedings three times a day, and her fur was no longer rough looking, but thick and probably warmer. "Hey, we have Snowflake with us today. I know you can see him. He's a wonderful dog and I know you'll love him, too."

Holly slowly stood up, not wanting to startle the dog. "There. Come and eat, okay?" she said, smiling into the dog's golden-brown eyes.

Backing off, she moved to Nick's side, watching Lady swiftly move to the bowls. To her surprise, she lapped up all the water in the first bowl. "She's thirsty," Holly said.

"Yeah," Nick murmured. He heard Snowflake whine. The dog stood at his right leg, unmoving, his gaze riveted on the yellow Lab scarfing her food down. "I'm glad we can do this for her. The Bitterroot River is nearby, but the edges of it are frozen ice. It would make it tough for Lady to go out on that ice to try and get to some water to drink. It could break and she'd drown. I worry about that."

"Me too. Did you see how close she came to me?"

He smiled a little. "Yes, that's a good sign. There's no question that Lady was abused by a man or men. She's trusting you more and more every day, Holly."

"I would give anything to get her into my apartment and let her live with us."

He watched Lady gulping the food, not even chewing it. That was a sign the dog had been starved. "Let's take one step at a time," he murmured. "I'm not sure she'll ever feel safe enough to move into a building. She might feel trapped and not have an exit. That could make her go wild."

Nodding, Holly said, "I just feel so sad for her, Nick."

He slid his arm around her shoulders, drawing her against his left side. "You're the chief softy in our family."

She chuckled, and happily pressed up against him, loving the feel of his arm around her. "You have a heart of gold, too, Conway, and I know that." She gazed up into his eyes filled with adoration. Her lower body warmed because they had made love earlier in the morning. She had asked Nick to sleep with her nightly if he wanted. Even though they had two apartments, he spent most of his time over at hers.

She loved their shared evenings with Snowflake, either with the dog in the living room lying nearby, or later when they went to bed and he lay on his huge doggie bed in the corner of the kitchen. Most of all, she looked forward to long, searching talks with Nick, whenever an important subject arose.

"She's finished eating," Nick said, lifting his chin in the direction of Lady. "Now, she's interested in Snowflake. That's a good sign."

"Is it?" she asked, her voice hushed, her arm tightening a little around Nick's waist.

Snowflake's whole world was focused on Lady, who stood, looking torn between leaving and coming closer to where the couple stood. He whined, his stub and whole butt madly wriggling.

Nick lifted his arm away from Holly. "Let's see what Lady will do if I allow Snowflake to move closer to her on his leash. We'll do it slowly, so as not to startle her."

Holly stood, her gloved hands pressed to her coat, watching as Nick slowly crouched down and touched Snowflake's head. Then, he urged him to move forward with a command. Instantly, the dog started toward Lady. Nick kept his shepherd on a tight line so he wouldn't happily charge the Lab like a playful puppy. Holly pressed her hand to her lips to stop from making a sound of joy as Snowflake reached the end of his leash, straining, only two-feet away from Lady. The Lab stood there, eyeing him. And then, a miracle happened.

Lady wagged her long, thick yellow tail in slow, wide arcs.

Nick grinned and whispered, "Another good sign, Holly. She wants to be friends with him."

Lady came forward and pressed her nose into Snowflake's nose.

Both dogs wagged their tails even more vigorously.

Tears filled Holly's eyes and she rapidly blinked them away. "Oh, Nick! Look!"

He gave a low chuckle, nodding. "They like each other, but they're male and female, so that's part of the reason."

Holly stood watching the two dogs. Snowflake strained to sniff more than Lady's nose, but the leash prevented him from moving any closer to her. But Lady had no leash, so she walked up to Snowflake, sniffing his head, his neck, and finally, his behind. This was all doggy greeting and it made Holly smile beneath her gloved hand. Glancing down, she saw Nick watching them, satisfaction in his expression.

"This is so good!" she whispered.

"It is," he agreed, smiling up at her.

For the next five minutes, they watched the dogs introduce themselves to one another. Snowflake seemed to realize his normal bounciness and eagerness would scare Lady off. Instead, he stood very still while she sniffed him from stem to stern. Lady's tail never stopped wagging. Holly sniffed, wiping her eyes, overjoyed because Lady had so little and had obviously suffered so much.

Nick slowly pulled Snowflake away on the leash and Lady followed them.

"How close do you think she'll come?" Holly asked in a hushed tone.

"I don't know. We'll find out. She likes Snowflake, trusts him. You can see her looking at us, and then at him. She's probably figuring that if Snowflake likes us, we're trustable, too. At least, I hope that's what she's thinking."

"She doesn't look scared, Nick. She looks like she really wants to stay with Snowflake."

"Yeah, it's a really good sign." He stopped the leash at eight feet. Lady was now closer than she'd ever been to them.

"She's looking at you, Nick."

"Yes, I'm a man and a male hurt her. Did you notice she gives you a nicer look?"

Smiling a little, Holly remained absolutely still because she could see Lady studying them intently. Snowflake whined, straining to be close to her, but the leash prevented it. "She does look at me more warmly," she agreed.

A person walking past them on the wooden boardwalk suddenly startled Lady. She leaped away, whirling around, and scampering down the alleyway, disappearing.

"Oh," Holly cried softly, "she was so close to us, Nick!"

He rose and brought Snowflake to his side. Turning, he saw the man disappearing past the other brick building. "Yeah, but a stranger just walked by, spooking her." He smiled and touched her flushed cheek. "It's okay. We made huge inroads with Lady today."

"Can we bring Snowflake with us the next time we feed her? Tonight?"

"Absolutely. Lady likes him," Nick said, patting his shepherd. "You're such a handsome dude," he praised his four-legged friend.

Snowflake looked adoringly up at Nick, his stub wriggling nonstop.

Laughing softly, Holly moved to him, slipping her arm around his elbow. "Come on, it's cold out here. I'm ready for some hot chocolate. How about you?"

NICK STOOD BACK, looking at the blue spruce Christmas tree he'd just set up to be decorated. It was December fifteenth, and Holly was like a delighted child, hardly able to wait until he'd strung the lights around the six-foot-tall tree they had chopped down earlier in the day after getting a permit.

Outside, the afternoon sky was gray, warning of another snowstorm to come over the Bitterroot Mountains that surrounded the valley. This range was part of the massive Rocky Mountain chain and had been created from the panhandle of Idaho into western Montana where Hamilton sat. They were surrounded by steep, jagged mountains clothed in white winter raiment. It had always been Nick's favorite time of the year for many reasons. He and Holly had already had a tree trimming party over at his parents' home two days earlier. Now, they had their own tree. It was their first Christmas together and Nick's heart swelled with a fierce love for Holly. Since they'd decided to live together, he felt as if he were in some kind of unending dream.

He understood how important this tree trimming was for Holly. She had all her old childhood ornaments and things she and her sister had made in one box. Over the years, since having lost her family, Holly had made tiny wooden frames painted in Christmas colors, one for each member of her family. She would hang them on this tree so they could be with her and Nick. His heart ached for Holly's tremendous losses.

Snowflake sat nearby, watching them with interest. Sue had given Nick several of her prized decorations for their tree. These were things he'd made as a kid in the first and second grades, but still precious to his mother. He'd shared with his parents that he and Holly had decided to live together to see what they had would work over the long haul. Nick was positive that it would, but he didn't want to crowd Holly. Last week, he'd moved all his clothes and other items into her apartment, leaving his open for rental to someone else. His parents were approving.

Life was good, he decided, watching Holly as

she began to decorate the tree in the corner of the living room. He'd moved Snowflake's cushiony bed into the corner of her kitchen and his companion seemed very happy with the move, too. Besides, Holly was always giving him little treats, such as a slice of apple from a salad she was making, or a piece of meat left over from cooking. Yes, she was spoiling his dog, but she also spoiled him with her love. And Nick knew it was love. He'd never been happier.

"We're going to have Christmas Eve dinner with your folks," she said, placing a framed photo of her parents on the tree.

"I'm looking forward to it," he said. His mother had closed the diner for Christmas Day and Nick was glad. He didn't want her working if she didn't have to. Her husband, Chet, often helped out during the winter season because his tourism business, organizing fishing and hunting groups waned during that time and he could lend a welcomed hand to Sue. Coming over, he looked down into the large, cardboard box of Christmas decorations. All of Holly's family bulbs and other knickknacks were in there. Going over to her after she affixed another family photo to the tree, he urged her into his arms, their hips resting against one another. "How are you doing? I know this can't be a happy time for you, Holly."

He saw that her blue eyes were indeed sad with memories. Nick would give anything to erase them, but he knew no one ever could. Her family, all her memories with them, would come up at such times every year. He kissed her lips softly, feeling her arms go around his waist as she leaned into him.

Nestling her face against his chest, she closed her eyes. "I'm okay, there are just so many memories . . . good ones, Nick. Really."

He kissed the top of her head. She had pulled her hair into a ponytail and decorated it with some plastic mistletoe to hide the rubber band. She was so childlike in some ways, but it was opening him up, too. She invited spontaneity and it was something he thought he'd lost. Now, being with Holly was bringing some of the old Nick Conway back, she was breathing life into him once again. "You're my gift," he told her gruffly, tightening his embrace, feeling the curved softness of her body meet and melt against his own hard body.

"Oh, let's not argue over who's the better gift," she laughed, pressing a kiss into his red and black-checked flannel shirt.

Chuckling, he murmured against her temple, "Fair enough. What can I do to help you prepare for tonight?"

"Help me decorate the tree."

"It's been so long since I've been around one," he admitted. "Doing Mom and Dad's tree two nights ago seemed strange to me."

"That's because you spent so many years in Afghanistan instead of being home." She eased away but gave him a swift kiss on the lips. "Now, you're a civilian, Nick, and you are re-entering life as you knew it." She became somber, holding his gaze. "In my heart, I think you're so lucky to have your parents. I'd give anything to have mine back and to have Noelle here with us."

He caressed her cheek. "I know that and I wish I could do something to make it so, but I can't."

"I know . . . and it's okay. Every year it gets a little less painful for me." She walked over to the cardboard box. Holding up two paper angels that had been colored with crayons, she said, "Noelle and I made these. Her first grade teacher was the same one I got when I started school." Turning them around, she brought them over. "See? Mom put our names on them so she knew whose was whose," and she smiled sadly.

"Where would you like to put them?" he asked.

"High up on the tree. You're taller than I am, Nick. Could you put them just below the star at the top?"

"Sure, I can do that," he said, picking up the first one.

Standing back, she said, "Oh, that's a perfect spot for Noelle's angel!"

He smiled over his shoulder. "You know

she'll always be with you."

Holly felt her heart break with loneliness. "She was my best friend growing up, Nick. We did everything together. She never treated me like a little sister underfoot. We hiked the Bitterroot Mountains together, we caught trout in the river that parallels Hamilton. She taught me so much, but she never treated me like I was a pain in the butt."

"Those are good memories to always hold on to," he murmured, stepping back and taking her paper angel. "Want to be right beside her up there?"

Wanting to cry, but holding back the tears, Holly nodded, handing it to him, a lump in her throat. Wanting to move beyond her loss, she said, "I just finished the collar for Snowflake's Christmas gift."

Hanging the angel next to the other one, Nick asked, "Can I see it?"

Holly moved to her knitting bag and placed it up on the couch. Nick came and sat down next to it. "Actually," she said, giving him a worried look, "I made two of them." She lifted up a green knitted dog collar that had the word "Snowflake" in white yarn around it. "I know he can't wear this when you have him out on a leash, but I thought he might wear it for Christmas? Kind of his decoration for the season when he's indoors with us."

Nick liked the double thick collar. It had a simple loop and a button to close it up around the dog's neck. "Sure, why not? He'll look Christmassy," he said, smiling.

She took it and laid it up and over the back of the couch. Giving him a concerned look she said, "I made a second one, for Lady," and she pulled it out of her knitting bag. It was bright red with "Lady" in white letters. "I hope I got her neck size right," she said, handing it to him.

Nick grimaced. "You think we'll be able to ever get a collar of any kind on her?"

Shrugging, Holly said, "I do. She's trusting us more and more every day, Nick. I'm hoping that she'll come to me someday and she'll let me slip this on her. Everyone in town knows we're trying to tame her and they're all for it. Your mom thinks Lady will trust us because we love her. Dogs pick up on that. You know that more than most," and she smiled, watching him gently handle the two-inch-wide collar.

"This is a nice, thoughtful gift. I hope you're right. We've gotten close enough to her to see the way her fur is wrinkled around her neck. I talked to the county sheriff, Chuck Dandridge, about it and he said she was probably tied up with a chain around her neck for some time. The chain was probably so tight that as she grew, it actually cut into her flesh." Nick gave her a sad look. "At some point, I know someone either let her off that chain, or she broke it and ran away."

"But in breaking it," Holly whispered, "she had to tear that chain out of her fur and skin."

"Yeah," Nick answered grimly, handing her the collar. "Lady may be supersensitive to anything around her neck because of it. The way her fur lies around her neck now makes me think she won't want us to touch that area, much less place a collar around her. She's going to have bad memories about such things. I'm sorry."

"That's okay," Holly said, wrapping it up and tucking it into her knit bag. "Maybe someday."

HOLLY HELD HER breath as Lady, after gobbling her evening meal on December seventeenth, happily came toward her and Nick, with Snowflake beside them. By now, Lady was eager to see her new doggie friend and every day Nick took one more foot of the leash in, so that the Lab had to come closer and closer to them. Lady didn't seem to mind, but her eyes were always on Nick. He made no moves when she came to see his shepherd.

Holly had brought a piece of bacon left over from their last stop to feed their shut-ins tonight. It was wrapped in a paper towel. She had completely forgotten about it until Lady, who was no more than six-feet away from her, lifted her long nose, sniffing toward her, and picking up the scent. To Holly's surprise, Lady came shyly up to her left side, nose almost touching the coat pocket holding the bacon.

Nick gave her a questioning look. "What's she smelling, Holly?"

Dazzled by Lady's boldness she whispered in amazement, "I had a piece of fried bacon that I'd wrapped in a paper towel and put it in my pocket. I forgot to take it out when I put her bowl down in the alley earlier. What should I do, Nick?"

"She wants it. Lady trusts you. Slowly lift your hand and pull it out. Don't let her eat the paper, though. You're going to have to make some movements and it might scare her off."

Holly smiled down into Lady's golden eyes that looked so much clearer than ever before. Finally, her thick, winter coat looked sleek and none of her ribs were sticking out any longer. "I want so badly to reach out and pet her."

Nick laughed a little, a low sound so as not to startle Lady. "A step at a time. She's comfortable enough around us, especially you, so go ahead and give her the reward, that bacon."

Holly smiled nervously and followed Nick's directions. She had her gloves on and Lady watched intently as her hand slid into the pocket and withdrew the wrapped bacon.

Lady started wagging her tail. She took another step toward Holly, her gaze on her left hand.

"That's great," Nick praised, "you're doing fine. She totally trusts you, Holly. This is a breakthrough."

Thrilled, Holly pulled the fried bacon from the paper. She leaned down just a little, slowly easing the meat in her hand toward Lady's muzzle.

Instantly, Lady snatched the morsel, but instead of grabbing it and running away as she used to, she stood, licking her chops, looking for more.

"Ohhh," Holly said, smiling widely, "she loved it!"

"She's waiting for more. That's why she's not turning and running like she usually does."

Giving Nick a stricken look, she said, "But I don't have any more. What am I going to do?"

"Try to pet her head. Make your movement very slow so it doesn't spook her. Maybe she'll settle for a loving pat instead of a second piece of bacon you don't have," he said, grinning.

Her heart was pounding as she called, "Lady? May I pet you?"

Lady tilted her broad head, her gaze locked on Holly's. Her tail was still wagging.

Holding her breath, Holly slowly moved her hand and Lady stood, watching her. Even with her glove on, she could feel the thickness of Lady's fur. "Ohhhh, she's letting me pet her,

Nick!"

"That's great. Just keep your hand on her head because I don't know if she wants anyone touching her neck area."

For another minute, Holly patted Lady's head and softly touched her large, floppy ears, giving her pure love. The dog had relaxed, which amazed her. She continued to speak quietly to Lady, urging her to let her pet her more. The moment she lifted her hand, Lady backed off a few feet.

"Something's spooking her," Nick muttered, looking around. Sure enough, a teenager was walking past the alley. "It's okay, Holly. I think she's had enough for one day. Good work. This is real progress. We're going to start bringing Lady bacon. It's the next step to taming her. She'll do anything for that bacon. All Labs are foodies. They'll do anything for food," and he grinned broadly over at Holly, who was plainly moved by Lady trusting her enough to make physical contact with her for the first time. "This is an unexpected Christmas present," he said, holding Holly's beaming expression.

CHAPTER 7

December 18

HOLLY TRIED TO contain her excitement as Lady loped up the alley toward the three of them, her eyes alight with happiness. Snowflake was leaping around on the long leash like he had jumping jacks for legs. She'd found out early on that because he was a herd dog genetically, he needed a lot of exercise every day. Nick took him down to the Bitterroot River less than a quarter-mile walk from the charity, and threw him his favorite red ball until he was tired out. Even foot-deep snow that had fallen last week didn't stop the intrepid dog from chasing that ball along the bank of the river.

Snowflake's back was even with Nick's knees. He was compact, swift, and turned on a dime. Now, he was leaping joyously around on the leash as Lady came from the end of the alley toward where they stood.

Holly grinned over at Nick, who was also smiling as Lady loped easily toward them, her pink tongue hanging out the side of her mouth. "She's getting so much tamer," she said.

"Yes. It's the combo of bacon and Snowflake here," he said, laughing. In the last few days, Holly had brought bacon with her and Lady would gulp her food in the alleyway bowl, then come trotting up, say hello to frisky, playful Snowflake, and then move quickly over to Holly, waiting for her dessert—the bacon. Holly had been able to not only pet her head, but now, she was running her gloved hand across her back, staying away from the chewed up area around her neck.

The damage to that area had been done at least a year ago from what Nick could tell. Lady was still circumspect of him, still watching him, but he gave her no reason not to start trusting him. She was becoming more comfortable in his presence, although Lady clearly favored Holly for many reasons.

Lady happily licked Snowflake's face, smelling him front to rear, and then turned her attention to Holly, who laughed and warmly praised her. The dog wasn't pushy Nick observed. She was careful around Holly, as if she were delicate and might break if she made too much contact with her today. With Snowflake, she was robust, and gave as good as she got. Labs were a very athletic breed, too, and got along well with everyone because of their easygoing temperament.

"Are you ready to start our experiment?" Holly asked Nick as Lady gobbled the bacon from her hand.

"Yes." Nick called Lady by name. The Lab knew her name because her ears pricked up and she lifted her muzzle, looking directly at him. He held out a piece of fried bacon in his hand. Giving Snowflake the order to sit by his right leg, which he did, he called Lady again. She could see the bacon in his hand. And he could see she was torn, but the bacon won out.

Lady came tentatively toward Nick. He knew he was tall and probably looked threatening to the abused dog, so he slowly crouched. Snowflake remained at his side, unmoving as Lady approached. Talking softly to the Lab, he offered her the piece of bacon.

Delicately taking it, Lady watched him carefully as she gobbled. Once she got the bacon, she quickly backed off a good six-feet away from him, chewing it.

Nick smiled and kept talking to Lady in a low, persuasive tone. Her ears were up and her focus was a hundred percent on him. He reached down and pulled another piece of the bacon out of a Ziploc he had in his pocket.

Lady's ears perked up. She intently watched him.

Nick didn't have to do anything except offer it to the dog, who came right up to him, taking the bacon. This time, she moved three-feet away from him, still alert, but clearly enjoying the treat.

"She's trusting you," Holly called softly, smiling. "Finally."

Nodding, Nick said, "She's doing well." When the Lab was finished, he slowly produced the last piece of bacon, offering it to Lady. She came forward without fear, delicately taking the bacon from his fingers. Once again, she backed off.

"She's doing really, really well," Holly said.

"Sure is. I think time, Snowflake, and the bacon made the breakthrough," he said, giving her a boyish grin.

Lady came forward, touching Snowflake's nose. And then, she turned, looking toward Holly. Nick watched as the Lab hesitantly turned and walked slowly down the alley once again. About midway, she halted, and looked over her shoulder at them.

"She looks like she doesn't want to leave us," Holly said, hopeful.

"Yes, she's waffling."

Holly held her breath, watching the yellow Lab as she stood there, as if invisibly torn between wanting to come back to them, and leaving. Finally, her feral side won out and she walked toward the other end of the alley, tail tucked between her legs.

"I wish she'd follow us home. It's only half a mile to our charity. Think she would come inside our apartment?" Holly asked, hopefully.

"I doubt that," Nick warned. "She likes you and Snowflake, but she's still unsure about me. I wouldn't even try to get her inside our apartment because if she panicked, she'd tear it apart trying to escape. It's too soon to even think about that, Holly." Nick gave her a sad look. "Sorry, but this is a long-term kind of thing with an animal like Lady."

"But it's so cold out here, Nick!" she grimaced, "and late December in Hamilton, the weather is going to get below zero. I worry for her. She's a short-haired dog. I want so much to knit her a nice yarn coat that she could wear out here, but I don't think she'd let me put it on her."

Nick watched Lady, who again hesitated at the other end of the alley, giving them a long, yearning look. Snowflake whined and then looked up at him. "Does she want to come back with us, boy?" He leaned over, patting his shepherd's head.

"Why is she hesitating like that?" Holly asked.

"Dogs are pack animals," he said. "She's starting to bond with us, Holly. She doesn't want to leave her pack, but she's afraid, given her past. And fear is stopping her from fully trusting me, in particular. I think if you and Snowflake were here by yourselves, she might have followed you back to the van."

"She has to trust you, too," Holly said, watching the Lab. "We're together. We're not separating you out because you're a male and a male probably hurt her in the past."

"Well," he said, rubbing one of Snowflake's black and white spotted ears, "she's wanting to trust me. We don't want to know her past life before meeting us because it's probably pretty brutal. I saw dogs like this in Afghanistan. They're maltreated there all the time."

"Don't tell me," Holly said, holding up her hand. "I can't stand to watch TV commercials where animals have been mistreated. I have to turn off the sound and then leave the room."

He gave her a warm look. "I love your soft heart, Ms. McGuire. You stay that way, okay?" he teased.

Rallying, Holly saw Lady slowly go to the left and disappear out of their line of sight. "I wish we knew where she lived."

"I've stopped myself from snooping around," Nick said, now urging Snowflake to get up. He walked over to Holly, placing his arm around her shoulders, walking her toward the curb where the van was parked.

"Why?"

"Because if we find her nest, she'll have to move and never return to it. Lady has to have a sense of safety and if she smells me or Snowflake around it, she could feel threatened. She might think that I, as a man, have compromised her safe place." His mouth firmed. "So, I don't try to find her. She knows we're going to show up at this alley three times a day now and she's here like clockwork. It's as good as it gets." He squeezed her shoulders. "Get that worry off your forehead, okay? She's gained a lot of her lost weight back and she's getting fed well. Those things will help Lady not feel so cold even when the temp goes down."

Pouting, Holly muttered, "I don't care. No animal should be out in this kind of winter weather."

He opened the van door for her. "No disagreement, but the ball is in Lady's court, sweetheart."

She warmed to his endearment, sliding into the passenger-side seat. Nick placed Snowflake into the van and the dog came up to stand between the front seats. Holly petted his head, loving the gleam in his beautiful, blue eyes. "You really like Lady, don't you?"

Stub and butt wriggling, Snowflake whined.

Nick grinned as he slid into the driver's seat. "He's head-over-heels in love with Lady. Never mind she outweighs him, is taller, and longer than he is." He shut the door, turning on the engine.

"I don't think dogs see things like that," Holly said, smiling, rubbing Snowflake's thick, wiry fur across his back. The dog loved standing between the seats.

"They don't," Nick said. "But they do have likes and dislikes, even in a pack. Snowflake is an alpha male. And Lady acts like an alpha female. So that's part of the attraction."

"I wonder if she's spayed or not?"

"Probably not," Nick said. "A lot of redneck owners who abuse their dogs by chaining them up aren't thinking about such things."

"That's awful," Holly muttered, pulling her seatbelt across her body. "Is Snowflake fixed?"

"Yep. The Army wants their dogs, whether male or female, not thinking about breeding. They all get fixed so they focus on the job they're to do, not be distracted by hormones and such."

"That's good," she said. "I just wish pet owners would always be responsible like that. Too many aren't."

"I know," he agreed, turning the van around and heading out of town on sloppy, salty, watery Main Street. It was midday and the sky was turning gray with an oncoming front that was slowly moving into their area. The weather forecasters were warning of a major snowstorm across the Rockies. Because Hamilton sat on the east side of the mountains, they received a lot less snow, but they got the frigid cold.

"I really think we made huge steps with Lady today. Don't you?"

"Yes," he said. "Tonight after we get our shut-ins fed, we'll see if she'll duplicate that same behavior."

"I think I'll tell Myra to cook up some more bacon this afternoon," she said, smiling fondly, her hand resting on Snowflake's back.

"Well, Lady can use that extra fat because she's going to have to deal with below zero conditions this coming Christmas."

"I can't believe it will be that cold! The weather is changing so dramatically!" she exclaimed. "Did you know that our average temperature is eighteen degrees in the winter?"

"I know. And snow is accumulating a lot more this year than I've ever seen it before."

"This past summer, before you arrived home, we used to get around thirteen-inches of rain for the whole year. But we've had some hellacious fronts come through and dump a lot more than usual. The Bitterroot River flooded a couple of times because of thunderstorms in the mountains, and it all converged here, in Hamilton. No one has gotten flooded out—yet. But the weather is quirky and unpredictable."

Nick pulled into the charity parking lot and switched off the engine. "Mom was telling me about that flooding. Everything's changing, that's for sure. The forecasters are saying there's a string of lows coming in off the Alaska Gulf and it's going to deliver record-setting amounts of snow, along with off-the-charts temperature plunges."

"I worry about Lady."

"I know you do," and Nick reached over, lightly touching her cheek. "She'll survive because she's a survivor."

"But wouldn't she love a nice, warm room and a soft doggy bed like Snowflake has?"

"I'm sure she would," he said, opening the door. "Why don't you and Snowflake go inside? I'll load the dishwasher. I'll see you in a bit."

NICK WATCHED LADY quickly gulp her food, her shadowy form highlighted by a streetlight midway down the alley. It was around nineteen degrees out tonight and he and Holly were bundled up to ward off the sharp, gusty wind. Holly stood, moving from one foot to another, nothing but nervous energy. Nick knew she was worried about Lady freezing to death during Christmas week. Looking up, he saw a gunmetal-darkened sky promising snow fairly soon.

"Here she comes," Holly said, excited.

Nick watched the Lab closely. This time she

wasn't as tense as she approached. She came up without hesitation to touch noses with Snowflake, who was wriggling his stub for all it was worth, saying hello to her. Lady gave Nick a passing look, and he saw the wariness in her dark, shadowed eyes, but her body wasn't tensing up this time. All those were good signs as he watched the Lab go quickly over to Holly.

This time Holly crouched down on one knee, lifting both her hands, and patting Lady's head, shoulders, and body. The dog's tail was like a metronome broadcasting her happiness over being showered with such genuine affection from Holly. After petting her, she gave the dog her bacon, which Lady quickly slurped down, and then looking at Holly, silently asked for more.

Laughing, Holly slowly stood up, her hand on Lady's head. "No, I don't have any more, girl." She gestured toward Nick. "He has some for you, though. Go to him, girl."

Nick crouched down after telling Snowflake to sit, which he did. His partner knew what was going to happen next as he reached into his pocket and drew out a piece of bacon. He called softly to Lady, who turned, looked him up and down, and then willingly made her way over to him. She took the proffered bacon, standing, chewing it with relish, but not moving away from him as she had this afternoon. Nick was sure the dog was cold. And he could see her weighing her proximity to him. As he continued to talk to her in a low, soothing voice, he gave her a second and third piece of bacon. Making no attempt to reach out and touch her, he was surprised when she boldly came forward, her face almost in his, cautiously sniffing him. He remained still, allowing her to smell him from his head, shoulders, arms, and chest.

Nick understood what she was doing: familiarizing herself with his scent. What was going on in her dog brain right now? Was she tucking away his scent in her memory and putting it in the "safe" category? Or the "food" category? She wouldn't have come up and sniffed him at all if she distrusted him. She'd have backed off as she had so many times before.

"I think she's saying hello to you, Nick. That's the first time she's smelled you."

He gave a bare nod of his head, not wanting to startle Lady, who remained close, still testing the air around him. The Lab could smell one last piece of bacon he had tucked away in his pocket, and he grinned, keeping his eyes averted from hers. Dogs, like all other animals, often took direct eye contact as a threat or challenge. Nick wanted Lady to consider him part of the pack, but not the leader.

Lady moved to his left side, pointedly smelling, and making noisy chuffing sounds near his left pocket where he had the Ziploc bag with the last piece of bacon in it. He suppressed a chuckle, spoke quietly to her, and kept his movements slow as he retrieved it. To his surprise, she sat down, watching with great interest as he dug into the pocket, thumping her tail with anticipation. To sit down meant she felt a certain kind of comfort level with him, even though he was a man. His heart soared as he realized he'd built up her trust one meeting at a time, one piece of bacon at a time. Labs were gluttons when left to their own devices. They'd eat anything. And it was the lure of the bacon that had finally melted that barrier between her and him.

Nick didn't take Lady's acceptance of him lightly, however. They had a long road to go yet, and he wished that they were further along in their trust issues. That way, he might have been able to get the dog into the garage beneath their apartment and make her a much warmer and comfortable place to stay.

As he eased his hand out of his pocket and extended the food to Lady, she took it with great delicacy, sitting there, munching it with great relish, smacking her lips, her pink tongue on the move. Nick smiled as he saw the pleasure come to her expressive, gold face, her dark eyes glistening with pleasure. Wanting to reach out and touch her gently, he stopped himself. Snowflake, when off the leash and at the apartment, would come up for pats from him, sometimes nosing his leg or licking his hand. His shepherd wasn't shy about wanting that physical contact with him. He wondered if Lady would be the same. She finished off the bacon, licking both sides of her muzzle one last time. For a moment, she really looked into his eyes. Nick felt an energy, a probing coming from her, but couldn't define it.

Lady stood up, shook herself, and then wandered back to Holly. It was time for her to go. Lady said goodbye to her, came to Snowflake, touched his nose, and then stood there, staring up at Nick.

He didn't move.

Turning, Lady ambled down the alleyway again, with that same hesitation.

Nick tried to swallow his disappointment. A feral animal couldn't be forced into anything. It had to be on the animal's time, making it their decision, not his or Holly's. He knew how much she wanted to try and get Lady inside for this coming round of bad weather. She would worry herself to death about Lady. But there was nothing he could do about it. To reach out and try to place a collar on Lady, or in any way manhandle her to get her into the van and then take her to the garage, would shatter the trust that had been built up between all of them, tonight. No, they all had to be patient. Very patient.

December 23rd

HOLLY SAID GOODBYE to their last shut-in, making sure Mrs. Cannon had been taken care of. Nick stood out in the hall with the sack containing items that would be washed back at the charity. The first weather front had come through. It dropped only two-inches of snow, which wasn't much, but the thermometer went down to zero overnight. Always worried that her shut-ins would not be properly warm, Holly took extra time to ensure they had socks on their feet, sturdy knit slippers that she'd made for each of them for Christmas, and that their heating source was working properly.

Bundled up, they hurried to the van, Snowflake off the leash trotting at Nick's side. Gusting wind cut through the Main Street area. Holly noticed no one was outside in this life-threatening temperature unless they had to be. Worried about Lady, she compressed her lips and climbed into the passenger seat after Nick had opened the door for her. He stashed all the sacks in the back while Snowflake leaped in, taking his place between them. She patted his head, smiling into his darkened eyes, the blue color in them illuminated by a streetlamp near the vehicle. Her breath was white.

"This reminds me of Afghanistan," Nick growled, shutting the door and turning on the van. He cranked up the heater.

"The cold?"

"Yeah, we were stationed near the Hindu Kush Mountains and we froze our asses off," he grumbled, pulling away from the curb.

"What did you do for Snowflake?"

"I put protective, sheepskin-lined paw boots on him for starters. Dogs can get their pads frostbitten, and the type of work we did was always in rough, rugged country. He's got a really thick coat so I never put any cover over his back."

"Those paw boots sound like a godsend. I wonder how Lady's paws are holding up?"

"Well," he said, reaching out and squeezing her knee, "she's not out in this weather. She's hunkered down in her nest, wherever it is. Her paws will be tucked up beneath her body, so she'll do okay."

"This is just awful weather, Nick," Holly said, chewing on her lip, frowning as she watched the buildings as the van moved past them.

"Not nice," he agreed. "At least your shut-ins are all doing good. No heaters have broken down, there's ample propane or oil in tanks for others, so they'll be okay as this series of storms passes through."

"Can dogs get their ears frostbitten?"

He glanced at her as he drew the van up to the curb between the two brick buildings. "They can, but it's rare. Are you concerned Lady's ears might freeze tonight?"

She opened her gloved hands. "Yes, I am. I really worry for her out in this. I mean, you don't see any animals or humans out tonight, Nick."

"There she is," he said, pointing toward the alley. "Waiting for us."

"Oh, good!" Holly said, relief in her tone. She quickly climbed out, her boots crunching in the few inches of snow frozen on the sidewalk.

Nick gave her a tender look and kept the van on, wanting to keep the interior heated. They would be good and cold by the time they came back to it. He saw Holly slipping and sliding, arms out from her body to balance herself across the icy expanse as she went into the alley. Lady was already trotting up it toward her. Smiling, Nick placed Snowflake on his long leash, climbed out of the van, and grabbed Lady's dog bowl that he'd made up earlier. Tucking the other bowl under his arm and grabbing the quart of warmed water, he called his shepherd out of the van, and then slid the door shut. Snowflake was leaping around and Nick laughed as they made their way around the vehicle and over to the sidewalk. The stars were out, huge, twinkling globules in the ebony-velvet, night sky.

He watched where he was walking, balancing the bowls and water, and holding on to his dog's leash. To his delight, he saw Lady come up to Holly, wagging her tail wildly, licking her gloved hand, really glad to see her. She leaned over and gave the dog a hug, her arm going around Lady's neck. For a moment, Nick hesitated, expecting the dog to jerk back or react. But Lady didn't, much to his surprise. Holly kissed the top of her broad head, hugged her again, crouching in front of her, running her hands all over her long, lean body.

Nick didn't want to scare Lady, so he approached slowly, well within her line of sight. The Lab saw him and looked up, unwilling to leave Holly's warm, loving embrace. The cooing sounds of love she was bestowing upon Lady made her gold eyes glisten.

Nick saw Lady wag her tail at him in a friendly fashion. He told Snowflake to sit and his dog obeyed. Placing the leash holder next to him, he left a good six-feet between himself and Holly. Placing the food down, he stepped back, calling Lady to come and eat.

Nick watched Lady come over without hesitation and swiftly gobble all the dry food, plus some bits of leftover pot roast that Holly had sprinkled over the top of it. He filled the water dish, setting it down. Lady eagerly thrust her muzzle into the water, slurping happily, drinking all of it, nearly a quart of liquid. With this kind of icy weather, Nick knew there was no place for Lady to get water. It was all frozen.

He assessed her beneath the lights, paying

particular attention to her paws. Large balls of ice had formed between her toes. That meant she had been out, traveling around. Those ice balls could cause actual damage to her pads if they weren't allowed to melt off. They would get larger and larger the more Lady moved around the snowbound area. Nick wished she would come home so they could take proper care of her in this kind of deadly weather. Maybe the Spirit of Christmas would urge her to trust them enough to do that, but he didn't hold out much hope.

CHAPTER 8

December 24, Christmas Eve

HOLLY TRIED NOT to worry during the wonderful dinner that Nick's parents had shared with them at their home that evening. They had traded Christmas gifts to be opened tomorrow morning. Holly had knitted his parents sweaters to keep them warm during this unusually frigid weather. It was a gift that would keep on giving for years to come. She had also knitted Nick one, and it was now lying wrapped beneath their tree. By the time they arrived back at their apartment, the wind was gusting at forty to fifty miles per hour. It shook snow off trees surrounding the valley, the glittering, powdery snow filling the air like confetti. While it was beautiful to look at, Holly was concerned about Lady's welfare under such brutal weather conditions.

Once back inside the apartment, she realized

it was already eight p.m. Nick had made sure Snowflake's bed was in one corner, and he added water to the nearby bowl that Snowflake drank from. The shepherd leapt into his warm, cushiony doggie bed, giving Nick a grateful look. He'd been fed scraps of ham from the Conway dinner table and his tummy was full.

Holly saw that Nick was concerned about Lady, too, but said nothing. It would do no good to talk about how low the temperature was going to drop tonight. There was nothing they could do, and she hated this helpless feeling.

"I'm going to take a bunch of old blankets down to the garage," Nick told her, coming over, and sliding his arms around her waist.

"Why?" she looked up into his dark, green eyes.

"I think tomorrow morning, when we go over to feed Lady, we should try to get her to come with us. I'd like to be able to lead her that half-mile back here into the garage. I'm hoping she'll follow Snowflake. If we leave the door open, she can see that we're not trapping her and that she can escape if she wants. We can feed her there and she'd have shelter out of the wind and something warm to lie on."

"I like that idea," Holly agreed. "I'm so worried about her tonight, Nick. I just feel awful."

"Yeah, I'm not happy about it either." He kissed the top of her head and looked into her eyes. "I know you're worrying, but Lady is a fighter. She survived any number of winters before this. And we've been feeding her regularly and she has a layer of fat on her now. It will act as a barrier for her."

Holly slid her hands up and down his arms, feeling his quiet strength. How she loved him! "I know. I keep telling myself that."

"I'll be down in the garage, trying to set something up for Lady that she'll accept. You might let Snowflake out when he needs to do his nightly thing."

"I'll take care of it," she promised. Nick had trained Snowflake weeks earlier to go to a specific corner of the parking lot near the bushes and grass, to do his doggy toilet before going to bed. All she had to do was let the shepherd out when he walked up to the front door, letting her know he needed out.

"Okay," he said, giving her a swift kiss on the lips. "I'll be back in about half an hour," he promised.

There were many things to do to get ready for Christmas morning breakfast for her shut-ins. About fifteen minutes later, she saw Snowflake leave his bed and trot down the hall toward the front entrance. Drying her hands on a towel, Holly knew it was time to let him out. Snowflake stood expectantly at the door.

Leaning down, she patted his head. "It's cold

out there, big guy, so make it fast, huh?" and she smiled, opening the door. Outside, it was dark except for the lights in the parking lot below. The wind was savage, tugging at her corduroy pants and sweater. She watched Snowflake gallop down the passageway toward the stairwell. There was no way she was going to stay out here and watch him as she usually did. He knew what to do and was well-trained. As she turned, she thought that in about five minutes, he'd be back, scratching at the front door to be let back in.

Closing the door, Holly hurried back to the kitchen. She wanted Christmas morning breakfast to be special for her elders. Never did she want to live alone, as they did. She wished mightily that she had a single building where all of them could stay together, but the money wasn't there to make her dream come true. Until then, it was ten stops at ten homes to see each of them, which was better than nothing.

She was so busy collecting the pumpkin muffins that she'd just taken out of the oven that she didn't hear Nick coming in until the front door opened and closed.

He sniffed happily. "Mmm, those muffins smell good. I've got Lady's new home all arranged," he told her, coming over and kissing her forehead. "Can I steal one?" he grinned, reaching for one of the muffins.

She slapped his hand. "No way! There are

exactly twelve there—one for each of our elders, and one for each of us for tomorrow morning's breakfast."

Nick chuckled, his hand on her shoulder. "All right, oh keeper of the muffins."

She laughed.

"Where's Snowflake?" Nick asked, looking around the kitchen.

"Oh my God!" she cried out.

"What?"

"I let him out fifteen minutes ago!" Holly said, hurrying to the door. Opening it, she didn't see Snowflake. Nick came and stood at her back, his hand on her shoulder. "I let him out and he never came back," she said, her voice rising with concern. Twisting a look over her shoulder, she looked up at Nick. "Why isn't he back? He always comes to the door when he's done his business."

Nick frowned and shut the door, leaning over the ice-cold railing, looking down into the parking lot. "I don't know. I was down in the garage, but the door was closed. Maybe he heard me down there?" Nick gave a sharp whistle. It was one that Snowflake recognized as a signal to come to him.

Holly wrapped her arms around herself, terror coursing throughout her. "I don't see him, Nick. Why isn't he here? Could he be down at the garage door? He might have heard you earlier and gone there, instead."

Nick turned, placing his arm around her hunched shoulders. "Let's get inside, it's too damned cold to stand out here without winter gear on."

Inside the foyer, Holly could barely contain her worry. Nick quickly shrugged on his jacket, a knit cap, mittens, and gloves.

"You stay here in case he comes to the door. I'll be right back. I'll bet he heard me down there and he's sitting outside waiting to be let in."

"I hope so," she whispered, giving him an anxious, apologetic look.

The door closed.

Nick came back ten minutes later, scowling. "I can't find him. This makes no sense. He's never taken off on me."

"Where could he be?" Holly asked, watching him shrug out of his winter jacket.

Shaking his head, Nick muttered, "I have no idea."

"God," she whispered, "what if he scratched at the door when he was done and I just didn't hear him, Nick? Would he take off, then?"

"No way. He'd sit right there and wait for you. He knows this is his home," he countered grimly.

Holly bit her lip. "I have such a wild imagination, Nick." She reached out, gripping his upper arm. "What if Snowflake was down at the edge of the parking lot, near the highway? What if someone saw him and picked him up in their car? What if someone took off with him?" Her voice was scratchy with fear as she searched his darkening features.

Nick was just as flummoxed as she was. The way his mouth tightened made her want to cry. She felt guilty. Snowflake meant the world to Nick. He'd often told her that his shepherd had helped him survive in so many ways. He loved Snowflake with his life.

"No, I don't think it would happen. First of all, at this time of night, no one is on the highway. It's too damned cold, Holly."

Rubbing her brow, she squeaked, "What if there was a cougar passing by? You know they're in our valley here."

Nick stared up at the ceiling for a moment and then lowered his chin, holding her gaze. "Anything's possible, Holly. It just makes no sense. He's a WMD trained dog. He knows where home is. He knows he's to be with me at all times. I don't think he'd allow someone to pick him up."

"Can we call the police? Let them know he's missing?" she suggested, fear entwined around her words.

"Yes, we can." Nick shook his head in utter frustration over this development.

Holly could just see the look in his expression, as if this couldn't be happening. More guilt ate at her. "I'm sorry, Nick. I'm sure he scratched at the door." She made a helpless gesture down the hall toward the kitchen. "I was rushing around. Trying to get those muffins baked," and she sniffed, wiping her eyes. "I didn't hear him. Oh, God!"

"Hey," he murmured, folding her into his arms, holding her tightly, "this is not your fault. Stop feeling guilty."

Just then, there was a loud, continuous scratch at the front door.

Nick quickly released her.

Holly looked toward the door. "Snowflake?"

"I don't know . . . I hope so," Nick said, opening the door.

Gasping, Holly's eyes went wide. There, standing in the doorway was Snowflake and beside him, Lady. A cry lodged in her throat, her gaze swinging toward Nick, who was frozen in place as he surveyed the two dogs.

Before Nick could move, Snowflake walked right in and Lady followed close behind him, nose to tail.

Holly, stunned, watched as the shepherd took Lady down the hall and right into the kitchen. Dumbly, she looked up at Nick, who had the same befuddled expression on his face. "Snowflake brought Lady to us, Nick," she said, her voice trembling.

Shutting the door, Nick stared down the hall. "I wouldn't believe it—except it just happened," he muttered, shaking his head.

She heard the utter relief in his voice and saw how happy he was that his dog was back. "What do we do now, Nick?"

"Hell, I don't know. It sounds like they're both drinking water right now. He must have gone to where Lady was hiding and led her back here." Scratching his head, he gave Holly an amazed glance. "He's a herd dog, Holly. He sees Lady as a part of his herd and he has a responsibility for her—that's all I can come up with!"

She moved to him, hugging him fiercely. "It's a miracle."

"I hope so. I'm worried Lady will bolt if she gets scared."

"She didn't look frightened when she came in," Holly pointed out.

"She's trusting Snowflake." He looked down at her. "Can you go into the kitchen first and get some of that bacon you fried up? Make her up a little bowl of food so she knows she's to stay with us. That might help ease her worry about being closed in with no place to exit if she gets scared. She trusts you, Holly."

"That's a good idea," she murmured. "Where will you be?"

"Right here. Let me know when she's done eating and I'll show up at the entrance to the kitchen."

"But she didn't even look at you this time, Nick. It's like she knows this is her home."

Giving her a half grin, Nick said, "Yeah, I saw that, too. I don't know what to think."

"Dogs have their own language. Maybe Snowflake told her she was safe here and not to be afraid of you?"

"That would be nice if he did, Holly." He listened for any other noise emanating from the kitchen. There was none. "It's quiet in there," he said.

"I'll go to the kitchen," Holly promised, quickly moving down the hall.

When she turned the corner, she halted, pressing her hand to her mouth to stop from laughing. Taking a step back, she gestured to Nick. "Come here. It's all right."

His brows fell as he quickly walked down the hall to where Holly stood. "What?" he demanded, turning.

"Look," she whispered, smiling and pointing into the kitchen.

Nick halted, disbelieving. Snowflake lay on his big cushion in the corner. Lying right next to him was Lady.

She thumped her tail, giving both of them a look of hello.

Snowflake panted, a relaxed, happy expression on his face.

"I'll be damned," Nick rasped, sliding his arm around Holly's shoulders. "He's brought her in and made her part of his pack. Somehow he knew when she'd be ready to accept us, too."

Laughing softly, Holly smiled up at him. "What a Christmas gift, Nick!"

"Yes," he said, giving her a look of disbelief, "Lady is Snowflake's gift to us."

"To all of us, I think." She slipped her arm around Nick's waist. She could feel his shock over what had just happened. "The water bowl looks empty. I'm going to go fill it," she said. "Come on, come with me to get the bacon out of the fridge. I don't think Lady is going to bolt and go anywhere."

Nick wasn't as sure, but moved slowly to the other corner where the food mat was located, the water and food bowl on it. Leaning against the counter, his arms across his chest, Nick watched the two dogs. Lady was now licking her paws, pulling off the collected ice balls that had clung to the fur between each of her toes. He watched Holly fill the water bowl and set it back down nearby.

Instantly, Lady bounded off the dog cushion, coming to her side, eagerly lapping up the water. Holly cooed to Lady and patted her thickly furred back. The dog wagged her tail in response.

Nick was flummoxed. Giving his shepherd an amused look, he said, "You could have at least let us know where you'd taken off to, Snow-flake."

Snowflake lifted his head from his paws, head cocked, his blue eyes sparkling with doggy laughter.

An unwilling smile tugged at Nick's mouth.

"I'm going to give her a little dry food and a few pieces of bacon," Holly told him, her hand on Lady's head as both dogs looked his way.

"Good idea," he said. "I'll stay where I am. I don't want Lady to feel uncomfortable with me in such close proximity."

"Okay," Holly said, walking past him, Lady walking casually at her side.

Nick watched Holly open the fridge. The Lab lifted her nose, sniffing, catching the scent of the bacon as Holly took the container out of the fridge.

When Holly walked to the counter beside Nick, he wasn't sure what Lady would do. The dog came and sat next to Holly, watching her peel open the plastic lid, knowing full well what was inside it. What amazed Nick was that the newcomer didn't even send him a wary look. How could that be?

Holly then went to the broom closet on the other side of the kitchen, Lady walking with her once more. She put a couple of handfuls of dry kibble into Snowflake's bowl and took it back to the counter. Sprinkling about six pieces of bacon over it, she smiled and asked, "Are you hungry, Lady? Come on," and she took the bowl to the food mat.

Leaning over, Holly placed it next to the water bowl and stood back, watching Lady swiftly zero in and start gulping down the meal. She wagged her tail as she ate.

Holly moved over to Nick, placing her arm around his waist, leaning against him, watching Lady. "This is just amazing," she admitted, smiling up at him. "She's not afraid anymore, Nick. She's really comfortable in here."

"Probably due to Snowflake," he agreed, squeezing her shoulders.

Lady slurped with her pink tongue, turned, and wandered back to the cushion, lying down on it about six-inches apart from Snowflake. She continued to work on getting the rest of the ice balls removed from between her toes.

"Wow," Nick murmured, "this is such a shock."

"A good one," Holly agreed. "Why don't we leave them alone so Lady can get used to the sounds and smells of our home and to us? Snowflake's already asleep."

Snorting softly, Nick said, "He ran half a mile in that cold to find her and then another half-mile back here. He's got to be whipped." He pulled Holly around and led her to the entrance, turning off the light switch, the area drenched with darkness. "Come on, let's take a shower together. We've had a long, stressful day, too."

NICK AWOKE SLOWLY on Christmas morning. Light was peeking around the drapes, telling him it was at least seven a.m. They had an hour before they had to get their elders fed. Lifting up on one elbow, he tenderly watched Holly continue to sleep. She had worn her pink, flannel granny-gown to bed, the ruffles around her neck tangled in strands of her red hair. His heart burst with so many fierce feelings of love for her that he knew he'd never be able to put them into words.

He didn't want to wake her, but knew he must. They worked as a team to get the elders fed and he knew they were all awaiting their delicious morning meal that Myra and Holly had prepared for them.

He'd left the bedroom door ajar, just in case he heard either dog whining or barking. Normal-ly, he wouldn't do that because Snowflake slept out in the kitchen and they slept in here. Hearing a soft whine, he looked over his shoulder at the edge of his side of the mattress. Snowflake's blue eyes danced with a "good morning" to him. He was wriggling his butt in welcome. Smiling, Nick eased away from Holly and reached out, patting his dog's sleek head.

Lady's head popped up. Surprised, Nick grinned as the big Lab, who had been curled on his side of the bed, unwound and stood up. She stretched out on the rug.

"Good morning to you too," he said, laughter in his voice. Lady had apparently accepted him because she came over, wagging that thick, whippy tail of hers, standing next to Snowflake. Her eyes were gold-hued, and he could see what looked like pure joy radiating out to him.

Holly stirred and murmured some words he couldn't make out. Sitting up, Nick turned his attention to her as she struggled upright, the bedcovers falling around her waist.

"Are the dogs okay?" she asked, her voice hoarse with sleep as she scrubbed her eyes.

"Oh, I think they are. Take a look over on my side of the bed," he suggested, his voice tipped with humor.

Holly scooted over next to him. "Oh!" she cried out. "They're both in here!"

Lady instantly moved toward her, and Holly lifted her hand and leaned across Nick in order to pat her head. The Lab came forward, licking her fingers hello, her tail wagging furiously.

"How did they get in here?" she asked sleepily, sitting up, pushing the hair away from her face.

"Remember I said I was going to crack the door open when we went to bed, just in case one of them started whining or wanting out?"

"Oh," she said, scooting out of the bed, "that's right. They must have come in sometime during the night to sleep with us."

Nick climbed out of bed, being respectful of the distance that Lady gave him as she backed off a bit. At least she didn't look wary of him. "They both slept on the braided rug over here on my side of the bed," he told her.

"Why don't you feed them while I get a quick shower?" she asked, halting at the door to the bathroom.

"Go ahead," Nick said. He knew Holly would need at least three cups of coffee and a hot shower to wake up. She was a deep sleeper, unlike him. But then, she didn't have PTSD, like he did. As he padded barefoot to the other bathroom down the hall, both dogs following him, he smiled. Just sleeping with Holly nightly was helping his PTSD to dissolve even more. Sometimes he got nightmares, but they were coming fewer and further between, because of her. He loved her. And Nick could hardly wait for when they had their own breakfast later here at the apartment. There was a special surprise he had for Holly. What would she think? How would she react?

After a quick shower, Nick dressed and made his way into the kitchen. No surprise that each dog was on either side of the food mat, waiting expectantly for food. Grinning, he told them, "I need another dog bowl!" Lady thumped her tail and Snowflake's butt wriggled. Both dogs looked rooted to the food mat. Nick wondered if Snowflake had told the Lab that this was where he ate daily.

He turned on the kitchen oven to two-hundred degrees Fahrenheit and put all the aluminum containers that held breakfast for the elders into the oven. He'd warm them upstairs, instead of in the oven in their charity kitchen. It would take half an hour for them to be warmed up. He put the ten pumpkin muffins into another container. There was a lot to remember to take along for their meals, so he did that first.

Then it was time to feed the dogs. Nick decided to take the other six pieces of fried bacon in the fridge and divide them equally between the two dogs. Lady got twice as much kibble as Snowflake, but she was an eighty-pound dog beside his fifty pounds. For the first time, Nick got a good look at Lady's ruffed up neck area, seeing how the fur was twisted. He leaned over within six-inches of her, sliding the bowl in her direction. She did not flinch, nor did she have a distrustful reaction to him.

It was a Christmas miracle indeed, Nick decided, giving Snowflake his bowl of kibble with the bacon over the top of it. Searching through a cupboard, he found a huge, heavy plastic salad bowl and filled it with water. While the dogs ate, he set it between them.

As he prepared Holly's crucial morning coffee, he enjoyed hearing the sound of the dogs eating nearby. Checking the clock, he knew Holly would be out of the shower shortly. Flipping on the switch for the coffee, he started getting the two oven warmers prepared. As he laid them out on the table, he heard Holly come in.

"Mmmmm, the coffee smells wonderful."

"It's almost ready. Hey, look at the dogs."

Holly stood near the sink and poured the coffee when it was ready, cup in hand, watching them eat. Lady had already finished and was slurping down the water from the makeshift bowl. "She's so happy, Nick."

He lifted his head after unzipping the two warmers. "So are we."

"Is she wary of you at all?"

"No. I haven't tried to pet her, though. I'm going to leave that up to her. Now, I need to get them outside to do their morning business."

Holly smiled as he called both dogs and they left their emptied food bowls, trotting smartly after him. She loved the clacking of their paws on the wooden floor as he took them to the door.

"I'm going out with them," Nick called to her. "We'll be right back."

"Wear a coat!" she called. "It's freezing out there, Nick." She heard him laugh as he opened the door and then, a scrambling of doggie feet, and the door shutting. Pouring herself another cup of coffee, she saw that Nick had the food warming in the oven for their elders. She sipped the hot, black coffee, humming happily. First, they would feed their shut-ins, make sure they were warm and safe, then come home and make their own Christmas breakfast. Outside, snow-flakes were twirling and falling, but the nasty, cutting wind was gone. It was a perfect, Christ-mas-card morning!

CHAPTER 9

NICK TRIED TO still his anxiety as he and
Holly finished up their Christmas breakfast
at ten a.m. All the elders had enjoyed a wonderful
breakfast earlier and were grateful, but missed
Snowflake, whom they loved to pat. Holly
explained about Lady coming indoors, and they
all wanted her to come with Snowflake to be
loved and adored, too. Nick promised that in
time, if Lady wanted to come along, Holly would
introduce the Lab to them.

Outside, it was fifteen degrees below zero
and nothing stirred outdoors. He had kept
Snowflake at home in the apartment with Lady in
order to keep her company so she wouldn't panic
at being closed in, without any visible escape.

When they arrived back at the apartment, the
two dogs were in the living room near the
fireplace that had died down to red, glowing

embers. Then, Nick had taken both dogs out to do their business. Once they were finished, they were more than happy to race back into the apartment and get inside where it was warm. He'd rebuilt the fire and they remained close to it.

Holly had put on Christmas music and was humming away as she set the table for him. He had cooking duties today and made them a festive omelet of red and green, chopped sweet bell peppers, some shredded, sharp-cheddar cheese, and a touch of crushed basil leaves.

"Lady is really making herself at home, don't you think?" Holly said, coming and leaning against the counter near Nick.

"Yes, it has kind of taken me aback. I guess I expected her to continue to be wary of me, but she doesn't seem to be." He flipped the huge omelet over in the skillet.

Holly placed the plates next to the stove for him. "I think she made up her mind a few days ago that you were safe and could be trusted," she said. "When she smelled your face, neck, and shoulders, it was as though she was imprinting you into her heart."

Happily, Nick cut the omelet in two, placing half on each of their awaiting plates. The toast popped up and Holly quickly buttered the sourdough bread, adding it to their plates. "I'm just surprised, is all. Glad, for sure. I know Snowflake has been the role model for her, and that's a big positive. He's the alpha male in their relationship, so it makes sense she would follow him wherever he goes. Ready to eat?" He topped each of the omelets with a dollop of sour cream.

"I'm starved!" Her eyes twinkled. "Besides, after we eat, we get to open presents!"

"You're such a child," he teased, pulling her chair out for her to sit on.

"And I bring out the child in you," Holly laughed, sitting down.

Nick noticed that Snowflake came in with Lady. Both dogs went to Snowflake's bed in the corner of the kitchen. The shepherd liked his scraps put in his doggy bowl after they ate. Smiling, Nick sat down at Holly's elbow. "So as a kid, did you sleep at all the night before Christmas?"

"No, I never did. I was always getting up, sneaking downstairs to peek from the bannister to see how many packages had been left under our tree." She gave him a wistful look. "They were all good memories."

"Well, we're starting a new Christmas morning routine for ourselves. I know it can't replace your family, but," and Nick pointed his chin in the direction of the dogs, "we have our own four-legged family with us now."

"And that's wonderful," Holly assured him, smiling at Snowflake and Lady. "One of the gifts under the tree is a knitted dog collar for her. I know she's touchy about the middle of her neck because of the past, but I did something special for her collar."

Nick dug into the tasty breakfast. "I've seen you working on it in the evening."

"Yes, I made it a lot larger so that it will lie at the base of her neck and against her shoulders. I made it real loose. I thought we might be able to get it on her tomorrow when we saw her in the alley, but now, that's all changed."

"Yeah," Nick chuckled, "she came home to us." He saw Holly's eyes dance with merriment.

"Maybe after we open our gifts we can work with Lady and try to get her comfortable with that special collar. It's very lightweight. And I sewed on a red felt backing so that it wouldn't twist or pull out of shape."

"Sure, but you know, Holly, she's your dog." Nick knew because he was male that Lady would always have some distrust of him. "I'll just talk you through how best to do it, all right?"

"Okay. You really think Lady isn't going to eventually like you, too?"

"She might. We don't know her past or how damaged she was by a man or men. I hope she will. She gets along so well with Snowflake; they act as if they're inseparable."

"Sort of like us, huh?" she asked with a shy smile.

His heart thudded with love for her, grateful

for the gleaming look in her blue eyes that told Nick she loved him. His throat tightening, he reached out, squeezing her hand. "Yes, just like us."

"Maybe Lady came into our lives as a symbol of what is to come," she mused. "I always believed in synchronicity. Snowflake went out and got her yesterday because he knew how cold it was. He must have known she would trust and follow him to our apartment, that everything would be all right for her."

Nick gave his shepherd a warm look. "He's scary smart. There were so many times in Afghanistan when I could literally feel our minds joining one another when we were out on patrol. I could feel Snowflake thinking, shifting, and analyzing what was around him, whether it was safe or dangerous."

"I have that same connection with Lady!" she said, amazed. "When we're together, I can feel her. Literally, I can, Nick. That's just incredible!"

"That's why I said she's your dog. You two clicked with one another from the first time you laid eyes on each other." He smiled, finishing off his breakfast. "Are you about ready to open gifts?" he teased, knowing full well, she was.

"Yep," she said, popping the last of the eggs into her mouth. "Let me get us coffee first, okay?"

"Sure," he said, standing and taking the plates from the table. Nick made sure he'd left a bit of his egg and toast for both dogs. He had brought in Snowflake's secondary water bowl, which would be Lady's food bowl for now until he could buy her a proper one for her size after Christmas.

HOLLY POURED THE coffee, watching as Nick placed the tidbits into the two bowls. He called the dogs over and they leaped off the bed, scrambling across the kitchen to their food station. She laughed, handing Nick his coffee after he put the plates and flatware into the dishwasher. "Well, that was gone in three seconds."

"Doesn't last long," he agreed, sipping the coffee. "Ready?"

"Yes, let's go," Holly urged. She called the two dogs and they happily followed them out of the kitchen and into the living room. She sat down and placed her cup on the nearby lampstand next to the sofa. Lady sat on her right, Snowflake on her left. Nick brought up the gifts, laying the one for Lady near her. He placed a large box wrapped in silver foil and red ribbon into Holly's lap.

She felt excitement sizzling through her as

Nick sat down nearby, all the gifts distributed. He seemed so much lighter. Happier, maybe? "You go first," she said.

Nick opened up a gold, foil wrapped box. Inside was a knitted, dark-green sweater. It was thick and heavy, well made, and he drew it out, settling it against his chest. "I think it fits," he said. "And I can sure use it. Thank you."

Reaching over, Holly smoothed it out. "Perfect. It goes with the color of your eyes. Did you realize that?"

"No," Nick said, "but I believe you. This is going to get a lot of wear." He reached over, kissing her gently, threading his fingers through her loose hair. "I'm afraid what I got you isn't handmade by me," he said, drawing away from her, motioning to the box sitting in her lap.

"Oh, no worries about that," she said, tearing into the wrapping.

Laughing, Nick said, "You take no prisoners, Holly." And she didn't, ripping the paper apart with the joy of an excited child.

Holly gave a squeal of delight, her lips parting as she drew up a smaller box. "A camera!" she gushed, giving him a look of disbelief.

"A real one," he intoned, trying not to grin. "You were always taking photos of our elders, of me, Snowflake, and pretty landscapes with your cell phone. I talked it over with my mom one day and she said you'd been pining away for a camera but didn't have the money to get the one you wanted." His voice lowered with emotion. "She said you wanted a Canon D7 camera. That's what it is, Holly. Now you can take great photos for your Delos website and your blog."

Holly set the box on the coffee table after standing. She went over and sat on his lap, wrapping her arms around his broad shoulders. "You are so magical to me, Nick Conway! I love you so much!" She crushed her lips against his, kissing him long and deep, hearing him groan in appreciation as his arms wrapped tightly around her. As his hands ranged across her back, she pressed herself totally against him, luxuriating in his masculinity, as his mouth took command and sought hers with equal hunger.

Finally, they separated. When they did, both dogs were standing in front of them, wagging their tails.

Nick laughed.

Holly giggled. "Look at them! See that look in their eyes? They know we want to go make love!"

"Well," Nick said, his smile growing as he reached beneath a pillow at the end of the couch, "let's wait until after you open this gift." He produced a gold, foil-wrapped gift box with a red ribbon on it. Placing it in her hand, he settled Holly into the circle of his arms so she could lean against him as she opened it. "What? You're not going to rip into it like you did the other one?" he gloated, smiling up in her gaze.

"This is an awfully small gift, Nick." She carefully looked it over between her hands.

"My mom always told me the best gifts came in the smallest packages. Go ahead, open it, sweetheart."

She gave him a warm, caressing look and settled back into his embrace, never happier than at this moment. Her lips tingled and she could taste Nick on them. She just loved his male scent—she could never get enough of it. "Any hints, Conway?"

"You gotta be joking. You're too smart, Ms. McGuire. You'd ferret it out with your clairvoyant powers if I ever gave you the slightest of hints."

She snorted and kissed his brow. "Spoilsport," she chanted as she thoughtfully pulled the tape off it, untied the bow, and set them aside. When she opened it, there was a blue velvet box and Holly swore it was the same color as her eyes, or almost. A gasp escaped her as she held it up to him. "This is a ring box!"

Gently easing it from her fingers, Nick said, "It sure is. Come here, lean up against me. I'll open it for you." Holly nestled into him, her body fitting against his. Prying the box open, he turned it so she could really see what was inside.

"Oh!" Holly cried, her hands flying to her

mouth, her eyes huge as she stared down at the wedding-ring set. "Oh, Nick!" She turned, looking down at him.

"What? You don't like them?" he asked, suddenly feeling unsure.

"No . . . no, are you kidding? I love them! They're beautiful!" She began sobbing with pure joy, burying her head against his, her arms wrapping around his neck, holding him so tightly.

Nick didn't expect that reaction. He closed the case and set it aside, wanting to hold Holly, whose tears were soaking his neck and shoulder. Sliding his hand against her back and shaking shoulders, he thought that maybe, because she had lost her family, she never expected to marry.

Nick simply didn't know why she'd had that reaction, and wasn't about to go there. Holly was easily touched, there was no question. But he'd never had her cry like this, the sobs wrenching and so deep, tearing up and out of her soul. He buried his face in her sweet-smelling, red hair and rocked her gently in his arms, wanting to soothe whatever pain she was feeling. And it was clear to Nick that it was pain.

Gradually, the tears dissolved and she became quiet, her head nestled against his neck and jaw. It felt good to be able to give Holly the love that she wanted. "Better?" he asked, pressing a kiss to her temple. He felt her nod, heard her swallow several times, her breath still ragged with emotions.

"I never want anything more than you. Do you know that, Holly?" Nick squeezed her gently. "You're my new life—the life I've always wanted, but never dared dream about. It's you. You're like a beam of light into my dark heart. Your smile, your laughter, your thoughtfulness, they pierce my soul, and it's healing me a little at a time. You need to know these things. I know we don't talk on this level very often, but you're healing to me and I hope I am healing for you, too."

Holly slowly withdrew from her position, lifting her head, sitting up more. She pushed her hair away from her face and scrubbed the last of the tears off her cheeks. All the while, her moist, blue gaze was on Nick.

"Do you know what I love about you, Nick? There are so many things about you, about how you treat me, love me, care for me . . ." She sniffed and took the tissue he offered her. Blowing her nose, she crumpled it in her hand. "You do heal me, Nick." She slid her hand through his short hair, giving him a trembling smile. "You're my family now."

And then, she looked at the two dogs who sat like little Buddhas in front of them, expressions attentive but filled with so much love for them. "Snowflake and Lady are now a part of our growing family."

He nodded, swallowing against a lot of rising

emotions. "We are a family whether we realized it at first or not, sweetheart. Those rings? I didn't buy them for you to pressure you. I like living with you. We're three months into our relationship and I know it's early to think about such things, but I just feel that solid with you, Holly. You can take your time about us, about the possibility of marriage, someday, to me. I just needed you to know the depth of my commitment to you . . . to us, that's all."

She gave him a tender look, cupping his face, leaning down, kissing him slowly and with all the love she had in her heart, for him. Lifting away from his mouth, she whispered, "I can't wait to wear the engagement ring, Nick! I don't see anything but good coming from us meeting and falling in love with one another."

Nick tried to hold onto his escaping emotions, gazing into her warm, blue eyes, feeling her hand pressed against his cheek. He took her hand, kissing the back of it. "Then, let's see if it fits. My mom took a guess on your ring size because I couldn't ask you." He gave her a shy grin.

Holly reached across him and retrieved the velvet box. "I understand." She sat up and opened the box once more. "I just love that the engagement ring is a blue diamond."

"I wanted to get one that matched the color of your eyes," he said, holding it up. "It's not quite a match, but close."

"I love that you did this for me," Holly whispered, holding out her left hand toward him. "It's perfect!"

To Nick's utter relief, the ring slid easily onto Holly's finger. And it was a perfect fit. His mother was pretty good at this stuff. He watched Holly move her hand, the light playing through the blue diamond bracketed by two clear, smaller diamonds on either side of it. Her fingers were slender and she was so graceful, looking at the stones, pleasure wreathing her expression. "Do you like them?"

"I love them," Holly said, a catch in her voice. She leaned over, kissing him again. "I love you, Nick Conway. Forever."

He caught her hand in his, squeezing it. "Then, when we go over to my parents' home for dinner tonight, will you wear the ring?"

"Absolutely. I know they'll be happy for us, Nick."

"They sure will be!"

Giving the dogs a loving look, she said, "We are so lucky to have Snowflake and Lady, too. They are gifts to our hearts."

"They complete us," he agreed. She snuggled back into his arms, content to lie against him. "This is the best Christmas I've ever had," Nick admitted, looking up into her half-closed eyes.

"The best," she agreed. "And Snowflake's

gift of bringing Lady to us was another good sign, too."

Nick smiled at the dogs, both fully attentive, both with a happy expression on their faces as they listened to their humans talking in a language he was sure they didn't understand. But dogs understand emotions and can sense them easily. "Lady will always be your dog, Holly. Just as Snowflake will be mine."

"They are the best of friends, no doubt," Holly said, reaching over, patting each dog's head. "We have a journey ahead with Lady, but I know she's happy with us as her new family. There's some training to be done, I'm sure. I knitted her that oversized collar and maybe later we'll see if she'll wear it or not."

"Yes. And even if she's uncomfortable with it, you can keep working with her to desensitize that area of her neck so she can eventually wear it."

"She's so good at following Snowflake around, and she comes when I call her."

"We've got lots of good, quality Lab to work with," Nick agreed. "And this time around she'll be loved by us. Love heals. And over time Lady will forget her nightmare past and realize she's in a home where she's loved."

"And spoiled rotten," Holly said, smiling.

"You spoil me," Nick said, holding her luminous gaze, "so why wouldn't you spoil everything and everyone else around you, too?" Holly had a huge, giving heart and Nick felt like the luckiest man in the world.

"I think," Holly whispered, kissing his temple, "that we're all being spoiled by one another, but when you love like we do, it just happens naturally."

He kissed the hand wearing his engagement ring. "Forever," Nick promised her, his voice low with feelings. "Forever."

Lady whined and both of them looked over at their yellow Lab. Then, Nick's heart thudded hard. He couldn't believe his eyes. Lady was giving him a doggy smile that looked exactly like Dude's, teeth and lips in the same big grin. Tears filled his eyes.

Lady got up and walked around to his left side, sitting, head cocked, and Nick reached out slowly, gently patting her head as she thumped her tail. She smiled again. It broke him wide open with the grief he'd long held for his loss of Dude.

How could Lady know? Nick had long suspected that dogs were aware of humans and their mass of emotions. He'd seen it so often with Dude. Now, Lady, the same breed as his WMD dog, was reflecting her own emotions to share with him. They were sharing an understanding and Nick heard Holly sigh with joy.

"Oh, Nick! She's smiling just like Dude did in that photo you have of him! This is so wonderful! She loves you! She truly does!" Laughing, she leaned over, patting Lady's head, making cooing love sounds as the Lab happily thumped her tail.

He wiped his eyes. "Yeah, she knew, Holly. Somehow, Lady knew about Dude and how he'd smile at me, showing me his love." Shaking his head, he couldn't control the shock, the warmth, the opening, and healing of his heart that was triggered by her doggy smile.

"Not only will we help Lady to heal, Nick, she's going to help you heal from all the grief you buried when Dude died. She loves you just as much as she loves me. You've got to agree."

Nick continued to pet Lady, silently thanking her for her heart and her love for him. "Yes, I agree," he choked out. He wrapped his arms around Holly, burying his face in her silky hair, holding her, wanting nothing more than her, ever. "It is the best for all four of us," he agreed gruffly, tears running down his cheeks. "Just the best!"

THE BEGINNING...

Don't miss Lindsay McKenna's novella *Never Enough*, 3B1, Delos Series, about Matt Culver and Dara McKinley.

Only from Lindsay McKenn and Blue Turtle Publishing.

Available wherever you buy eBooks. Paperbacks are available through CreateSpace/amazon.com, and audiobooks through Tantor Media!

Read the sneak peek of *Never Enough*!

Excerpt from

Never Enough
by Lindsay McKenna

"**I** CAN HELP."

"Nope," he said, releasing her, heading for the doorway. "You just get comfortable and think about what you'd like to do with the rest of our day."

She helped Matt to put their clothes away once he brought in the luggage. The windows were open, and there were birds singing outside. A cooling breeze wound through the bedroom, and she could smell the plumeria. After she finished putting her clothes away, she walked over to Matt, placing her arms around his shoulders. A moment ago he'd looked so intensely focused on his unpacking, but as soon as she came and moved her body against his, sliding her arms around his neck, she saw an instant change, and it warmed her heart. She loved affecting him so powerfully. His gold-brown eyes grew amused.

"Uh-oh, I'm being stalked," he murmured,

turning around and taking her mouth, sliding against her lips.

The world halted. When Matt devoted a hundred percent of his attention to her, Dara felt like the most desired and cherished woman in the world. She loved kissing him, feeling the passion barely restrained in his kiss as he controlled himself for her sake. Moving her hips suggestively against his pelvis, feeling how thick and hard he already was, sent an instant ache and need of him through her.

"Mmm," she said, easing from his mouth, drowning in the gold intensity of his narrowed eyes. "Now you make me want to stay right here and love you instead of seeing Oahu."

He smiled a little, moving his hand down her supple spine, the red dress beautiful on her. "Up to you, sweetheart. I'm easy either way. We're on vacation, and we can do exactly what inspires you."

She liked being in his arms, leaning against his hard body. "We just had a ten-hour flight, and I'm jet-lagged. Are you?"

Shrugging, Matt said, "Yes and no. In order to adjust to Oahu's time, we should stay up." It was nearly noon according to his watch. "Hungry?"

"Well," she laughed, enjoying his hardness against her belly, inciting her, making her want to go nowhere, "my body is on East Coast time."

"Then," he said lightly, cupping the cheeks of her butt, moving her sensually against him, "let's do something easy, something that isn't going to drain us further."

"Such as?"

"Let me drive you down to Waianae. It's a pretty seacoast town, nice restaurants, the beach is nearby. You could kick off your sandals and walk in the sand or the ocean itself if you wanted."

"I like that idea. I love the ocean."

Matt slid his fingers through her mussed hair, watching the highlights glint beneath the lamplight above them. "Then let's do that. We'll be lazy today, just kick back, relax, eat when we're hungry, rest when we're tired."

The Books of Delos

Title: ***Last Chance*** (Prologue)
Publish Date: July 15, 2015
Learn more at:
delos.lindsaymckenna.com/last-chance

Title: ***Nowhere to Hide***
Publish Date: October 13, 2015
Learn more at:
delos.lindsaymckenna.com/nowhere-to-hide

Title: ***Tangled Pursuit***
Publish Date: November 11, 2015
Learn more at:
delos.lindsaymckenna.com/tangled-pursuit

Title: ***Forged in Fire***
Publish Date: December 3, 2015
Learn more at:
delos.lindsaymckenna.com/forged-in-fire

Title: ***Broken Dreams***
Publish Date: January 2, 2016
Learn more at:
delos.lindsaymckenna.com/broken-dreams

Title: ***Blind Sided***
Publish Date: June 5, 2016
Learn more at:
delos.lindsaymckenna.com/blind-sided

Title: ***Secret Dream***
Publish Date: July 25, 2016
Learn more at:
delos.lindsaymckenna.com/secret-dream

Title: ***Hold On***
Publish Date: August 3, 2016
Learn more at:
delos.lindsaymckenna.com/hold-on

Title: ***Hold Me***
Publish Date: August 11, 2016
Learn more at
delos.lindsaymckenna.com/hold-me

Title: ***Unbound Pursuit***
Publish Date: September 29, 2016
Learn more at:
delos.lindsaymckenna.com/unbound-pursuit

Title: ***Secrets***
Publish Date: November 21, 2016
Learn more at:
delos.lindsaymckenna.com/secrets

Everything Delos!

Newsletter

Please sign up for my free monthly newsletter on the front page of my official Lindsay McKenna website at lindsaymckenna.com. The newsletter will have exclusive information about my books, publishing schedule, giveaways, exclusive cover peeks, and more.

Delos Series Website

Be sure to drop by my website dedicated to the Delos Series at delos.lindsaymckenna.com. There will be new articles on characters, my publishing schedule, and information about each book written by Lindsay.

Quote Books

I love how the Internet has evolved. I had great fun creating "quote books with text" which reminded me of an old fashioned comic book . . . lots of great color photos and a little text, which forms a "book" that tells you, the reader, a story. Let me know if you like these quote books because I think it's a great way to add extra enjoyment with this series! Just go to my Delos Series website delos.lindsaymckenna.com, which features the books in the series.

The individual downloadable quote books are located on the corresponding book pages. Please share with your reader friends!

Made in the USA
Middletown, DE
14 February 2020

84698308R00109